The

Other

Wife

The
Other
Wife

Jackie Thomas-Kennedy

**PENGUIN
VIKING**

VIKING

UK | USA | Canada | Ireland | Australia
India | New Zealand | South Africa

Viking is part of the Penguin Random House group of companies
whose addresses can be found at global.penguinrandomhouse.com.

Penguin Random House UK,
One Embassy Gardens, 8 Viaduct Gardens, London SW11 7BW

penguin.co.uk

Penguin
Random House
UK

First published in the United States of America by Riverhead Books,
an imprint of Penguin Random House LLC 2025
First published in Great Britain by Viking 2025
001

Printed and bound in Great Britain by Clays Ltd, Elcograf S.p.A.

The authorized representative in the EEA is Penguin Random House Ireland,
Morrison Chambers, 32 Nassau Street, Dublin D02 YH68

A CIP catalogue record for this book is available from the British Library

ISBN: 978-0-241-72656-3

Penguin Random House is committed to a sustainable future
for our business, our readers and our planet. This book is made from
Forest Stewardship Council® certified paper.

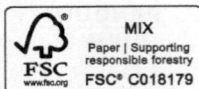

MIX
Paper | Supporting
responsible forestry
FSC
www.fsc.org   FSC® C018179

For M

I will go to X and say, "I'll let you have me," and he will laugh and say, "You're twenty years too late."

THE JOURNALS OF JOHN CHEEVER

I don't want to be older and wiser, I want to be younger and hotter: a love story.

MELISSA BRODER, SO SAD TODAY

The

Other

Wife

Prologue

ong before I settled in this part of the world, I was a guest, and everything was so unfamiliar to me that I had to be led: Here is how to buy the Metro-North ticket, and how to find your train. Here is where to sit if you want to see the river. My friend Claire convinced me that we should visit her parents, largely because we were sick of the campus salad bar. I was unprepared for how much I would covet the house I was about to enter, where some of the windows were stained glass and there was a fireplace, snapping with flames, in the dining room. The family served Pernod before dinner and played charades after dessert, which was a bowl of walnuts and clementines, the shells and peels left all over the table, because the cleaning lady was due at eight the following day.

When I came downstairs in the morning the lady was there, Claire's mother beside her, one washing, one drying, NPR on the radio. A cigarette burned in a pink saucer on the windowsill. Hip-to-hip, the two women chatted like friends. "This is Zuzu," Claire's mother said, introducing me. I didn't want to get too close to their maid. I saw that we used the same kind of bobby pins, although hers were at her temples, where her curls were gray, and mine were anchoring a loose twist. Instead of a handshake, I offered a nod and took my coffee outside, where I picked ivy out of the birdbath while I waited for Claire to wake up.

When I think of that evening—the tumbler glazed with Pernod, the sting of clementine juice on my chapped fingers, the way Claire and I cheated at charades—I recall feeling a smug certainty that I could have that life, inhabit a house like that one, with wainscoting in the kitchen and parents who delighted in their children. I believed that life was easy enough to find.

I believed this until we skipped Friday classes and took another train, this time to the city. We sat across from Claire's father, who bought us buttered bialys before he unfolded *The New York Times*. I'd never had a bialy before, and I devoured mine while Claire was inspecting hers for "too much onion." Until that point her father had left no meaningful impression on me, other than his general tidiness: He'd had his shoes polished while we waited for the train, and I could smell his aftershave. When he put on his glasses I saw that the case was old, its gilded letters mostly rubbed away.

As we approached Grand Central, he told us he'd have to run to his first meeting, several blocks from the terminal. He stood, briefcase in hand, and Claire tilted her head back. I did the same; I thought we were looking for something. In fact, she was waiting for her father to kiss her forehead, which he did, after which he kissed mine, a gesture of fairness and kindness, a good man's goodbye.

The kiss was chaste, dry-lipped, paternal, and brief; it had nothing of lust in it. It had nothing of my father in it either. The kiss promised me nothing, nothing, at a time when I wanted everything. The kiss said, *You can always visit*, and I did not want to be a visitor. When I opened my eyes I found my friend loathsome and spoiled. I saw that a comfortable life awaited her, that she would cycle out of this phase and into the next, that soon she would stand hip-to-hip with her cleaning lady while her husband rode the train. Everything she needed had already been gathered for her like a basket of kindling.

Claire and I lost touch decades ago, and her family moved away. If I ran into her now—say, at Grand Central, bialy in hand—it might surprise her to learn that I spent years in the town of her youth, that I chose it as the place to raise my son. I doubt she'd recall that moment on the train—that kiss she was used to receiving, a kiss she was happy to share. She couldn't know how it followed me; how, for some reason, every time I passed a shoeshine stand, I felt a warm blooming of my own potential; how, even after I married Agnes Blair, part of me wanted to know how it felt to have a husband who read the paper on the commuter rail.

I DID KNOW what it was like to have a wife who took the day's first train into the city. I knew what it was like to assemble the exact salad she'd asked for—to boil the eggs and slice the tomatoes, to whisk the olive oil into the lemon juice, to wash and spin the lettuce; to hear her say "I'm too tired to eat that, I'll just have toast"; to watch her leave the bag of bread open on the counter overnight, crumbs everywhere, twist tie lost.

I knew what it was like to become someone who cared, perhaps too much, about the lost twist tie on the bag of sourdough.

It turned out that even though I had chosen the house and the particular green of its newly painted shutters, I could still pace inside it, wondering why I was the only married woman on the block who ate alone every night. Agnes routinely texted from Grand Central as she ran to catch the 8:33. The firm reimbursed her for car service at that hour, but she preferred the train, which was bright and cold and better for work than a warm, private space that would have allowed her to sleep.

A fair question might be what I was doing with the time Agnes spent on the train.

She never asked me, and I never had to say that after the things I was proud of—quizzing Gideon on his beloved dinosaur facts over spaghetti; heating towels in the dryer for him while he was in the tub; lying in the top bunk, as he liked me to do, while he fell asleep below—I spent the remaining hours of the night tending to habits she rarely saw. At thirty-seven years old, I'd established an evening routine. I ate cinnamon toast and drank chocolate milk with lots of ice in the glass; I watched *Sex and the City* episodes I had fully memorized; I texted back and forth with James Cashel, my friend from college, who went by Cash, and whose wife was almost as busy as mine.

It turned out I could count the days since Agnes and I had touched each other. When I reached sixty, I saw it was better not to count. To remember what it felt like to lie next to someone who wanted me, I passed over Agnes entirely, even the first few years in New York. I resorted to earlier parts of my life, to the pre-Agnes window: the guy who stole limes from his neighbor to make me a gin and tonic; the one who hid my shoes in the sink when he wanted me to stay longer.

Cash, the first time and the second time.

I happen to know that I was thinking about this somewhat compulsively in the first week of February 2019. The texts are still on my phone. I initiated them after months of silence between us, attributable to being busy and to not having much to say. I texted him after three glasses of Riesling and a hot shower. Agnes was working in our bedroom. Gideon was asleep.

> ZUZU: how much do you miss me, scale of 1-10
>
> CASH: who is this
>
> ZUZU: very funny, what are you doing
>
> CASH: emptying the dishwasher
>
> CASH: for the first time in six years
>
> CASH: according to Molly
>
> CASH: who is sitting on the couch

CASH: also for the first time in six years
ZUZU: feeling sad for Molly
CASH: calm down I'm kidding

It was the first time he'd ever hinted at anything other than joy between them. I took a screenshot and tried not to read too deeply into it. I tried not to imagine, for instance, Molly hauling cardboard boxes full of her belongings down their narrow colonial staircase. I tried not to imagine him setting his wedding band, rather precariously, on the windowsill over the kitchen sink.

In the following weeks, I tried to get more out of him. I texted how are you and Molly, which was perfectly innocuous, but I also texted you'd better load that dishwasher and are you in trouble today. On February 5, 2019, I sent a message: bored bored bored bored bored. Only Cash would understand it, not because it was clever, but because it was the complete text of the first email I'd ever written him, nearly twenty years before.

That night, he had ousted me from his room because he was trying to focus. I had a paper to hand in too, at three the following day. I told him I was determined not to "waste time" grappling with deconstruction when I could do just as well if I wrote my essay five hours before it was due. I urged him to write his own essay tomorrow; I told him it would come out the same either way. "I don't think you understand how time works, Zuzu," he'd said.

Upstairs, in my room above his, I sent the email—*bored bored bored bored bored*—and an hour later he slid a CD under my door, a kind of apology. We had already established, by October, that he was perpetually indebted to me. At the time I found it flattering.

On February 5, 2019, he was perhaps not as charmed by my claims of boredom, and he didn't respond. I was cutting up a squash to roast for soup. I didn't want to finish cutting it, didn't want to sweep up the glistening seeds all over the board, didn't want to dig the immersion blender out of the cabinet. It was nine thirty, and Gideon was still awake upstairs, occasionally kicking the wall as he shifted in bed. I read a text from Agnes—still at client dinner—and set down the knife and the squash and lay on the kitchen floor.

I thought, *I hate this*, then waited for guilt. I was good at guilt. Lying on a hardwood floor I owned, under the glow of organic squash, was not a tableau that left room for much sympathy. I felt self-pity anyway, dirty and sweet. I felt it while I scraped the butternut squash seeds into my open palm. I felt it while I tried to remember the last time I'd had sex. The memory was of haste and quiet, not out of urgency, but out of obligation.

Upstairs, I checked on Gideon—finally asleep, green stars of light wheeling across his ceiling—and went into our room and sat on the edge of our bed. Agnes's nightstand held four empty water glasses and a stack of sealed envelopes, addressed only to her, that I had been adding to for weeks. She had recently claimed she didn't have time to "handle" her mail. I kept track of the bills and made the payments, but to manage her correspondence from bar associations and alumni groups, the occasional birth announcement, catalogues from stores she liked—this I refused to do.

I flipped back the duvet and settled against the pillows. I reread my last text to Cash—my "bored" sequence—and wondered if I was the only one who remembered that evening. I tried again: By the way, I totally understand how time works. He didn't respond to that either, at least not right away.

California Roll

~)

My sister was six months pregnant, and I had been making more of an effort to see her.

She had done the same for me when I was pregnant with Gideon and had once personally delivered a jar of homemade bone broth, wrapped in a dish towel for the duration of her journey from Springfield to Port Authority. At the outlet mall where we were meeting that afternoon, I arrived early and spent two hundred dollars on baby clothes. I sent Agnes a photo of the assorted onesies.

> ZUZU: do you think she'll like these
>
> AGNES: hard to say
>
> AGNES: but God love you for trying

As planned, Julia and I met in a handbag shop. She was wearing her blond wig, the one our mother hated.

"Auntie Z," she said, kissing my cheek.

"I got a present for the baby."

She stuck her hand into the bag and pulled a onesie halfway out.

"Green," she said. "Well. Just so you know, we're buying mostly purple."

"Noted," I said.

It was a difficult thing to shop with Julia.

The first time we met at the outlets, I bought six cashmere sweaters, three for Agnes and three for me, along with a four-hundred-piece train set for Gideon. Julia deliberated over a scarf, then left with nothing. *I guess you don't even look at the price tags*, she'd said. It was true. I hadn't.

The next time we met, I bought only a vanilla latte, and I complained about the exorbitant price. *Like you can't afford a coffee*, Julia said.

The seemingly obvious solution—one Agnes had offered, that very morning, without looking up from her phone—was that Julia and I should meet somewhere else. *Go for a hike*, she'd said. *Go to a museum.*

Julia and I were not from a go-for-a-hike family. Our mother, Trish, used to take us to the mall every Saturday. We tossed coins in the fountains and burned our mouths on hot pretzels. We got headaches from all the perfume. There was great comfort to be found in those massive, windowless caverns, looking down from the escalator at the polished floors. I could still feel it, as I watched my sister examine a leather bag smothered in logos: the thrill that was the potential of finding the right thing. The track lighting gleamed on her wig.

"You think this is tacky?" she said, setting the bag back on its stand.

"I think if you like it, that's all that matters."

"I already have it in black anyway. Perry got it for me." She flipped her hair over her shoulder and picked through a row of key rings. They looked like charm bracelets, with pink leather tassels and carved silver animals. She trotted a silver horse through the air toward me, whinnying.

"Buy me," she said, pressing the horse to my shoulder. "I'm on sale for forty-five."

"Tempting, but no," I said.

"Okay." She put the horse back. "I need to eat something, stat."

I tried not to make a face as we approached the food court, which smelled primarily of funnel cake and marinara sauce. A pigeon was trapped inside, flitting from one metal beam to another. Julia bought thirty dollars' worth of sushi; I bought a mineral water and a sea-weed salad I didn't want. We sat beneath a giant blue paper snow-flake. I watched her purple nails pinch the sides of the plastic lid, snap the chopsticks apart, arrange the ginger. Her hair was so long it brushed the sides of the table.

She pushed her tray toward me.

"Don't worry, my OB said it's totally fine to eat this. You want?"

I shook my head.

"Too good for outlet mall sushi?"

"Just not hungry."

She tapped her chopsticks against the side of the tray.

"Perry and I finally finished the second floor. Now we're just waiting on our living-room windows. And we have our first tenant."

She lifted a roll and held it close to her mouth. She loved to draw out her announcements. To reveal that she was carrying a girl, she asked Perry to film her slowly opening two clenched fists, revealing a piece of pink rock candy in each palm. I watched only half of it before handing my phone to Agnes, who said it reminded her of a music video she'd liked in high school.

"So? Don't you want to know who my tenant is?" Julia said now.

"Um. Is it Dad?"

"God, no. That would stress Perry out."

"Okay, I give up. Just tell me."

"It's Noel!" She paused, waiting, but I said nothing. "He's clean. He's quiet. Going through a divorce, you know."

"I had no idea," I said. "We're not in touch."

She broke her knob of wasabi into smaller pieces.

"He asks about you."

"Common courtesy."

"No, I mean *asks*. Like, *about* you."

"Did you tell him I'm happily married?"

"No." She tilted her head. The blond hair swung to one side. "Should I have?"

"Okay. I regret telling you that sometimes we bicker. Yes, Julia. You should have."

"Daddy needs a raincoat," she said, gathering her empty containers. "Come help me pick one out before all the stores close."

A grown woman, calling her father *Daddy*. I hated that.

THE SPORTING GOODS outlet maintained the aura of its regular stores. The walls were plaid and there was a canoe suspended over the registers.

"He says he doesn't need one," she told me as she pushed hangers along the rack. "I said Daddy, you can't just cover your head and run every time it rains."

I picked up a coat and put it back without looking at it. She wasn't seeking my opinion, and I had no idea what my father liked. I didn't even know his size. It annoyed me, the way Julia prattled on about him with that false exasperation; it was close to the way she talked about Perry, and the way our mother talked about Glenn. I pulled my phone out to see if Cash had texted back yet. He hadn't.

"You may as well reach out to him," Julia said. "Shit. This zipper is jammed."

"Reach out to who? Noel?"

"*Daddy.*"

"Did he say he wanted me to?"

"No. But obviously he would like more contact with his daughter."

"That's not obvious to me."

She held up two coats, one black, one red.

"You decide," she said. "Then I can tell him we picked it out together."

"What an honor." I touched the black coat. Julia nodded approvingly.

"He's not going anywhere, you know," she said as we stood in line. "He's sitting right there. You act like he's unavailable."

"I know where he is," I said. "Doesn't *he* know where *I* am?"

"Yes, but—"

"He has a grandson he's met, what, three times in seven years? And he wouldn't hold him the first two times because he was a preemie and therefore 'too small'? It's bullshit." I pointed at her stomach. "God knows he'll be holding her a lot more often."

"I hope so," she said. "And you should hope so, too, for my sake."

At the register, she hesitated, as if she were giving me the opportunity to pay, as if it were a privilege that I could buy this coat for my father. I pulled out my card. When the cashier offered the receipt to me, Julia took it. "In case he doesn't like the color," she said, folding the paper into thirds and tucking it away. I tried not to be annoyed with her. It was just a receipt. I thought of the bone broth, how carefully she'd wrapped it in her dish towel; how she'd made it after "doing some online research" about gifts during the first trimester; how, unscrewing the lid after Julia left, I gagged at the odor and pushed the glass of shaky amber away from me. Intercepting me at the sink, Agnes said she would drink it, that she couldn't bear the idea of all that wasted effort on Julia's part. I didn't think Agnes found it appealing either, but she drank it anyway.

Give Your Father the Coat

L ater, I would wish that I had found some reason to deliver
the coat myself.

There would have been no surprises, because nothing in
my father's duplex had changed since 1999. The TV would be on in
the living room, tuned to local news. Dinner would be either a rotisserie chicken or sausages, blackened in a skillet, served with rice
that came with a seasoning packet. The saffron-garlic powder in
those packets gave me heartburn; it gave him heartburn too. He
kept antacids on the mantel over his decorative fireplace.

I didn't like that he kept the antacids there, in clear view, as if
heartburn were part of life in his house. I didn't like that he kept a
beaded necklace in a dish by the microwave; the necklace belonged
to one of the women he'd dated after the divorce, and the way he
held on to it seemed desperate and sad. I didn't like the necklace, or
the saffron-garlic powder, or the way he sighed when he didn't know
the answer to the final question on *Jeopardy!*

I didn't like that he had skipped my quick, informal wedding
to Agnes, citing his discomfort with my "lifestyle." On the day we

married, he sent flowers, addressed only to me, to my mother's house. The card said, *Hope it was a pleasant day and all that you wished for.* Pleasant: a chaste, quiet joy. Not wedding joy, not the public outburst I thought a wedding was meant to be.

Had I brought him the coat, he might have asked why I spent so much on it. He would have thanked me. I would have wanted to leave within ten minutes of my arrival. I would have hated the way he doted on his cat, Betty, who preferred to spend most of her time under the drop-leaf table in his living room. I would have wished, within minutes of driving away, that I had figured out how to enjoy those hours in his company.

Casper's Eye

~_

Agnes called when I was ten minutes from home and asked me to pick up her take-out order.

"I have to make a U-turn now."

"So what? It's not that hard, Zuzu."

I let the phone drop into my lap. I tried the U, but still wound up making a three-point turn across two lanes of traffic, guided by the blasts of other people's horns.

The food was under my name, and when I glanced inside the bag, I saw that Agnes had ordered only for me: a single serving of farfalle with mushrooms, a spinach salad, and a scoop of stracciatella gelato in a take-out coffee cup. I felt guilty about my general irritation. I sent a text—thank you—and she wrote back Figured you'd be hungry after your time with Julia.

IT TURNED OUT that Gideon wanted my gelato, and after a few mild refusals, I agreed to split it in half with him.

"What'd you do today, G?" I said, handing him a spoon.

"Skate park." He pushed his sleeve up to show me a raw scrape and a neon bandage. "Then a slushie, then the comic bookstore. Also, I had a daymare."

I looked at Agnes, who winked. I hated bringing our son to the skate park, with its thunderous noise and older kids, but he asked to go almost every weekend. To take him there was a gift to me.

"Sounds like Mom kept you busy," I said.

"In the daymare," he said, mouth full of gelato, "I was stuck in a castle. A scary one, though, not a golden one."

I ran my hand through his curls. He ducked away.

"You have math homework that I want to see done, and back in its folder, before that TV goes on," Agnes said.

"But it's Saturday." He looked at me pleadingly. I had spoken too freely, of late, of my opposition to his frequent math assignments, and my feeling that children should not be tasked with turning into miniature versions of their overworked parents.

"Do your homework, dude," I said.

I MADE SO many mistakes that sometimes I prided myself on what I managed *not* to do; for instance, when I came into our bedroom that night, I expressed no surprise when I saw that Agnes was mending Casper, Gideon's stuffed koala. Casper had lost one of his glossy eyes almost eighteen months earlier. About once a week, Agnes said she would take care of it. *Finally*, I thought, but I didn't say it.

"So how was Julia?" A needle stuck from the corner of her

mouth. I was afraid to disrupt the bed and somehow pierce the inside of her mouth, so I sat on the edge of our paisley armchair, next to the clothes she'd left there.

"She didn't like the onesies I bought her."

"Why not?"

"They weren't purple."

Agnes laughed around the needle.

"What did you get?"

"Green."

"Green! How could you." She nodded at her tablet, which was charging on the windowsill. "What should we watch?"

"Our soap opera, obviously."

She lifted her knees under the blanket and propped her tablet against them. There was only one season of the poorly reviewed, historically inaccurate series about five polygamist families and their various entanglements. Agnes and I loved it, and we had tried to convince various friends of ours to watch it, but we were alone in our enthusiasm. It was one of the few things we were both willing to watch over and over. We had an ongoing joke: Agnes, who valued authority and respect, would want to be wife number one. We agreed that I would be better off as the newest wife, who was presumably the favorite, by virtue of novelty if nothing else. I wanted, above all else, to be desired.

I woke at two a.m., as I often did, and drank the glass of water I'd brought up to bed with me. I held my phone under the covers to block the light. I read my last message to Cash—By the way, I totally understand how time works—and concluded that he hadn't responded because he didn't know what I was talking about. I wrote never mind, then erased it, then put my phone underneath my pillow and faced the paisley chair.

Casper was in the chair, the repaired eye glinting with relief. I wondered if Gideon would still want his toy, or if, in its absence, he had determined that he was too old for it. Cash had sent it to him for his second birthday, a fact I mentioned often enough for Gideon to name the koala "Cash Bear." The first time he said it, I looked across the table at Agnes, whose only reaction was to sip from her glass of wine.

Later, when I asked her if she'd heard Gideon's name for the bear, she said, "Casper, right?"

"Yes, Casper," I said.

Agnes

September 7, 2007

Agnes and I met at a law school information session near Union Square. She sat two rows ahead of me, taking careful notes with a mechanical pencil that she clicked whenever a long silence fell. During a break, she unclipped her gold barrette and polished it on the hem of her tweed skirt. We wound up standing next to each other in the line for free coffee, and she turned to me and said, "I'm one of those kids who wore a suit when I toured colleges, and I didn't learn my lesson."

"I don't get it," I said.

"This." She gestured at her skirt. "It's too much."

"I think you look nice." I was pouring a cup for myself, but when I set it down to reach for the sugar, she took it.

We returned to our seats. I found that I was distracted by Agnes. Her low-heeled shoes came to an absurdly sharp point at the toe, and I glimpsed a magenta insole when she let her shoe dangle off her right foot. When an admissions officer asked if anyone already worked in the legal field, Agnes raised her hand and waved a little, and I saw the overeager student she must have been: the kind I'd always secretly envied a little, for how clear they were about what they wanted. I was in attendance only because my stepfather, Glenn, a trusts and estates attorney, had urged me to go. He'd offered to pay tuition for law or medicine. If I wanted to get my "PhD in crayons"— this was the phrase he applied to anything vaguely artistic—I would have to secure the funding myself.

At the end of the session, Agnes was waiting for me on the front steps.

"Susan," she said, reading my name tag, "do you want to get a drink or something?"

I suggested several places in Williamsburg. She'd never been to Williamsburg.

"What do you mean, never been to Williamsburg," I said.

"I live in my aunt's place on Central Park West," she said, shrugging. "It's free."

IT WASN'T A date, and neither were the next few nights we went out for drinks, all of them at a midtown wine bar Agnes knew because the first-year associates at her firm liked to go there after work. She ordered bourbon neat, or martinis; I ordered rum and diet soda. We both tried too hard to be funny. We laughed louder than people tended to laugh at that bar. Agnes made amends by ordering a sau-

22

cer of herbed olives. When I balked at the price, she said not to worry, she'd pay.

She seemed infinitely more adult than I was. She was a paralegal, and I was an editorial assistant at a small literary press that was always on the cusp of shuttering. Sometimes I left voicemails on the answering machines of poets I'd never read. I mailed out dozens of standard rejection forms each day, distressed by the cost of the postage. During my second year at the job, I raised my hand at a meeting for the first time and suggested that we ask submitters to enclose self-addressed stamped envelopes. "That's not how we do things," an editor said.

I disliked inefficiency. I disliked our garden-level office. My boss wore tight jeans and complained about his expensive divorce. The adulthood I imagined for myself seemed impossibly distant; there was no bridge to it, to the wainscoting and the stained glass and the Pernod, from where I sat. I lived with four people in a two-bedroom near McCarren Park, and although all of us could have produced our parents' credit cards in an emergency, we pretended otherwise.

At work, one of the editors—Ms. "That's not how we do things"—still used a typewriter, and the clacking sound suggested, to me, a refusal to change. I did not want to be stuck there, so far from what I knew to be possible.

AGNES AND I were LSAT study partners and midtown prix-fixe lunch friends; our favorite spot always brought petit fours with the check. I started picking her up after work once a week so we could get our nails done. She called my polish choices garish and I called hers boring; later, I saw it all as a reason to grab each other's hands.

On Saturdays we studied at a café near her apartment that played jazz and served chocolate and ginger scones. We were the youngest people in there by twenty years. I felt older around Agnes in a way that impressed me; around her, I felt the possibility of an important future, even if I couldn't quite grasp the terms of that importance.

"Assuming we get into the same school—which we obviously will—we could live together," she said one afternoon. Our study guides were so worn it looked like we'd dropped them in the bath and let them air-dry. She used fruit-scented highlighters that gave me a headache, but I didn't want to tell her. I was sick of studying for the LSAT, but I didn't want to tell her that either. She thought I was as smart as she was.

"We could live together," I said. "But where? You haven't come to hang out with me in Brooklyn a single time."

"How about this," she said. "If we do well on the test, we'll discuss it then."

THE NIGHT BEFORE our LSAT scores were released, we met for ramen near her office. When I turned west, toward her apartment, she suggested we go to my place instead.

"Finally," I said.

"You've never actually invited me, you know," she said. "All you do is bitch about how I never come over."

She punched my arm—an excuse for me to stop her hand, which I did, with my own.

AT MY PLACE I found two mugs and an open bottle of wine, which Agnes and I drank sitting side by side on the futon. The TV wasn't hooked up to cable, and the only DVD we had was a 1980s horror film neither of us had been allowed to watch when it came out.

"No way," Agnes said. "I can't watch anything scary."

"You can hide under this when it gets scary," I said, picking up a blanket.

"How long is it?"

"I don't know. Two hours?"

She set her glass on the floor, lay on her back, and dropped the blanket over her face.

"I'll see you in two hours, then."

"Oh, come on."

"I'm not joking. I don't want to have nightmares."

"You won't have nightmares."

"Sleep with me and you'll see," she said.

"You wish," I said.

Leadership

~⁓

We had a shelf over our bed. It held mostly framed photos of Gideon, and a few silver-threaded shells (that was Agnes; I saw no reason to keep a shell). Her parents sent us shot glasses with the Golden Gate Bridge painted on them, a nod to the view from Agnes's childhood home, and though it had started as a joke, we now slept beneath those too. Over time, the largest accumulation had become Agnes's awards from the firm: brass plaques, engraved sterling, etched glass. Heavy, sharp-edged recognition of her leadership, her dedication, her this, her that—she was good at her job, meticulous, rumored to read an email once and remember every word. She was so good that we slept beneath things that could crack my skull. (I mentioned this. She said I was being negative.)

At home, she forgot to pay bills and left the kitchen with the water still running. She left the cap off the toothpaste and her coat on the floor. In the first year of Gideon's life, she mistook a Sunday morning for a Monday four different times, then went into the office anyway. At home, she refused to plan, sort, budget, or reflect, unless it was in the service of an immediate goal. We paid ninety-nine dollars a month for a storage unit in Jersey City, for instance, because she didn't want to spend a Saturday sorting through our old stuff. We had been paying for it for almost eight years.

The unit was packed with things we would probably never use again—her flared-leg jeans, in every conceivable shade of blue; her undergraduate essays on Virginia Woolf; back issues of magazines that, inexplicably, she wanted to keep. Also in there, I believed, was a sweatshirt my father bought at a gift shop on Martha's Vineyard sometime in the 1970s. The navy cotton had faded, the white *M* was chipped, the neck was frayed, and the tag was gone.

I hadn't seen it in years, and by 2019 it was the only thing in that unit I still cared about. It had been beaten into softness that could not be replicated; you needed years to pass, you needed to wash it a thousand times, with a brand of detergent that had been discontinued in 1985. You needed to be my father, Dennis Braeburn, wearing it in all seasons, making chili in it, staining it with primer, standing too close to a fire and letting an ember burn a tiny hole in one sleeve. You needed to wear it as you gained weight and started to bald, so that one day you could give it to your scowling fourteen-year-old daughter, who had never been to Martha's Vineyard, and who was always cold.

Lump

When I woke at five thirty the following morning, Agnes was typing on her phone. I assumed it was work. I had learned, sometime around her second or third year as a lawyer, not to malign the firm on her behalf; she heard it as a complaint about her work ethic. Once, without looking up from her screen, she said, "You have no idea what would happen if I didn't answer this right away." It was true, I had no idea. She always answered right away.

She often responded to work emails at odd hours and went back to sleep, so I was surprised when she put the phone down and looked at me. She hooked her middle fingers together and turned them back and forth. At some point, stillness had been wrung out of her.

"Heidi wrote," she said. "She found a lump."

Heidi was Agnes's ex, and because they had maintained a friendship, I had been forced, on occasion, to sit at a table with the two of them, where I asked Heidi about her tattoos (some plants and their Latin names) and listened to her talk, at length, about her teaching job (health and botany) at a progressive boarding school. She had a long, long neck—good posture, Agnes later explained, from years of ballet—and she wore her purple hair shaved on the sides with a single thick curl in the center, each strand held fast with mousse. It looked like a dessert. When I met her, part of me wanted to lick her head.

"Sorry to hear," I said, skimming the newspaper on my phone.

I felt Agnes watching me. I could tell she was pointing and flexing her feet.

"I know she's not your favorite, Zuzu, but come on."

"What?" I put my phone down. "I said I'm sorry to hear it."

She pushed the covers away and stood up.

"Think about how nervous you were."

I, too, had recently found a breast lump, and it had required a biopsy. The nurse placed a pill under my tongue. It stilled my nerves, so that I murmured only "thank you, thank you" when the cold anesthesia spilled in. I couldn't feel the needle at all. I knew I was bleeding because I heard the nurse say something about how she was surprised by the amount of blood.

The results had come back benign—a relief, but there was still the aftertaste of a warning. Benign *this time*, was what I heard. Once someone says *benign* to you, you understand that at some point you might be back in the same chair, hoping to hear that word again.

"I mean, yes, I was nervous," I said. "I can tell Heidi that, if you want. It's not, like, an earth-shattering insight."

"Never mind," Agnes said.

I admired the imperious tilt of her head as she left the room. Self-righteousness suited her, and her sand-colored silk robe gave her a kind of royal effect. I stretched into the bed's empty space, vaulting my legs into the air and forming a kind of tent with the flat sheet.

Gideon had a tent in our living room, printed with dinosaurs, lit from within by fairy lights I'd wound around one of the interior posts. Years ago, on the afternoon I'd assembled it, I unzipped the window flap and declared to Agnes that it was too comfortable to leave, and that, for the foreseeable future, I'd be staying inside the tent. *Seems fair*, she said. Gideon was napping upstairs. She made us coffee and produced, from her favorite hiding spot behind the half gallon of milk, a pastry box with an éclair inside it, which we split, she lying outside the tent while I lay inside it, and we gossiped about people with whom we'd gone to law school, and with the soft cave light of the tent, the custard and chocolate on my tongue, Agnes's voice as she told a meandering story about a professor she'd liked, I felt younger than I was, for a moment, tucked away in a warm hold.

DOWNSTAIRS, AGNES WAS mashing bananas into pancake batter. Gideon was at the kitchen table, turning the pages of a comic book.

"Can I watch a show?" he said.

"Nope," I said. This was the standard answer in our house, except on Saturday nights.

"Start the day with positive energy, please," Agnes said, holding her sleeve out of the way as she dipped a ladle into the bowl.

Gideon opened the drawer where we kept the remote.

"Not now, G," I said, but he walked into the living room and flopped onto his beanbag. Soon I heard the theme song from his robot show.

"I give up." I reached past Agnes to pour a cup of coffee. "I really am sorry to hear about Heidi."

"Right. Okay."

"Has she seen a doctor?"

"Next week."

"Does she want you to go with her or something?"

"Heidi never asks for help, even when she needs it." Agnes, it seemed, was unaware of the warm approval in her voice. She licked batter from her thumb. "By the way, Reid's parents invited Gideon to go up to the Adirondacks with them over the long weekend."

"I know."

"Theresa called me *again*. We have to give them an answer." She came to stand behind me, setting her hands on my shoulders. "What do you think?"

"I don't know. Does he even want to go?"

"Apparently there's a pinball machine. And, according to Reid, a 'special oven for making pizza.'"

"And what would we do?"

"Sleep in! Go to bed early."

"He's so young, though," I said. "And the Adirondacks are so far away."

She sighed and dropped her hands from my shoulders.

"Your nerves are not a good enough reason to keep him from having adventures."

"I didn't say anything about nerves."

"I know you." She ladled batter onto the griddle. "We could get out of here that weekend. We could go check on Heidi. You could see Cash and Molly, too, if we're already over that way."

"Sure," I said, mostly because I didn't think Agnes would follow through with any of those plans. She often floated ideas while she cooked. More than once, I'd watched her put together an entire vacation while slices of red pepper fell from the blade of her knife. If I asked her about it later, she wouldn't know what I was talking about. I thought of it as a kind of productivity trance.

> ZUZU: might be in town soon, will you be around?
>
> CASH: I will arrange my schedule around your visit
>
> ZUZU: is that a joke
>
> CASH: why would it be a joke

First Orange

September 5, 2000

There was confetti all over the field, in the same shades of pink and gray as the shirts we'd been told to wear to orientation. My shirt hadn't fit over my breasts, but a guy on my hall, too hungover to stand in the sun, had offered me his. It was so long that it covered my shorts. The first thing James Cashel ever said to me was "That's not supposed to be a dress." The first thing I said to him was "That's not supposed to be your face." It was funny enough to us then. When it was time to pair off for a series of activities, I looked for him. He was already standing in front of me.

We did trust falls and helped each other through a spiderweb made of rope. When it was time to pick a brown bag lunch out of a milk crate, we both got in the vegetarian line. He ate his entire sandwich and a quarter of mine. We had a little battle with our celery sticks that we would both deny starting when I brought it up later.

After lunch, the juniors running the orientation told us to find new partners. I wandered among the crowd and ran into Noel Rafferty, who had, along with my sister and me, comprised the entire nonwhite portion of our high school's student body, and who joked that he'd chosen our college so that he could keep an eye on me.

All I wanted then was the pleasure of objectification—I wanted my name carved into someone's desk, wanted my name to change the course of someone else's blood. I wanted someone's friends to start teasing him every time I walked by. I wanted the things I forgot in my wake—my hair elastics and bitten pencils—to take on a totemic quality for one of the boys.

Not that boy though. Not Noel Rafferty. He was affable and uncool, and he wore his student ID on a lanyard. He looked like a tourist holding a map.

"I already know you, Noel," I said.

"So?" He pushed his curls back from his eyes.

"So the point of this is to meet new people."

I walked away from him, hands in my back pockets, the gold glitter polish on my toenails bright in the damp grass. Someone tapped me on the shoulder, and I frowned, expecting Noel again.

"We haven't met, right?"

It was Cash. Already, his voice was familiar.

"You were my partner ten minutes ago!"

He laughed, head back and eyelashes long.

"You're too serious, Susan. Anyone ever tell you that?"

All the time. I didn't say so.

We picked an orange from a basket. The fruit had to be passed from one person to the other for fifteen seconds without using hands. Some pairs were trying with the crooks of their elbows. Others, unwilling to touch a stranger, kicked it back and forth in the grass.

"I think it has to start here," Cash said, tucking the orange under his chin.

I stood on my toes and exposed my throat. My instinct was to hold his shoulders, but I kept my hands behind my back. The sun had warmed our faces, and I could smell only orange rind. His hair got in my eyes. When we fumbled, our mouths came close. There was little evidence of his orthodontia—later he would tell me he'd refused to wear his retainer—and there was an occasional gap or slight overlap among his teeth. It was the first time in my life that I bothered to imagine, specifically, the way a person's teeth would feel against my tongue.

The orange rolled from under his chin to the place I had made for it under mine. I gave it back to him. He returned it to me. Some-one blew a whistle. We won, he told me, grabbing my hand and swinging it into the air.

With our prize—a gift certificate to the campus café—we bought frozen strawberries blended with almond milk, which we drank on the library steps. When Noel Rafferty walked by and waved, I pretended not to see him. On those steps, with stained glass sparkling in the sunlight behind me, I believed that I could have anything I wanted. When my cup was empty, Cash took it and stacked it inside of his.

THAT YEAR HE lived one floor below me and claimed he could hear it whenever I paced. (Once, he slipped a note under my door: *You must have a test tomorrow.*) It was true that I paced when I studied, though I didn't study much. It was too tempting, and too easy, to run down a flight of stairs and burn CDs and eat with Cash. I learned to like the snacks he kept, the rice crackers and nori sheets and dried sour cherries.

He'd taken a year off between high school and college, and this impressed me. During his year off he'd worked as a landscaper in Connecticut, where he was from. He could make stir-fry, and had brought with him a contraband hot plate and a wok; he rigged these on his windowsill, window wide open to avoid setting off the smoke alarm. Even so, I had to stand there frantically flapping a textbook in each hand—he called this move "the deranged albatross"—while he fried presliced mushrooms and microwavable rice. We laughed hysterically every time we made our illegal dinner. Later, back in my room, my hair smelling strongly of sesame oil and garlic powder, I thought of how much I wanted to share his uncomfortable, standard-issue, metal-framed twin bed with him.

I could not help it: I was charmed by his idiosyncrasies. He drank black tea instead of coffee. He wore a red Patagonia vest in all weather. He put a stolen STOP sign on his door when he was studying. He made fun of people for listening to Top 40 radio, but he was generous with mixes, burning them for anyone who showed interest in music. Once, when we were high, I watched him play solitaire and dip cucumber spears in a jar of almond butter, occasionally offering me a bite without a word, and I took each bite even though I disliked the combination: It was the closest we seemed able to bring our mouths at the time. Our apparent need to touch each other embarrassed me even as it happened: We had thumb wars, we stole each other's hats. We frequently stood back-to-back to see who was taller, a question that did not ever need to be asked. I am not tall.

Denny or Trish

June 10, 1997

One of the local colleges sold passes to its indoor pool during the summer months. Our parents surprised us on a rainy day, telling us to put on our bathing suits and find our goggles. We went so early we had the whole place to ourselves. Our mother told us to stay in separate lanes, an attempt to prevent our constant bickering.

I was fourteen, Julia thirteen. We tried to synchronize our cannonballs off the diving boards. We screamed for the pleasure of the echo. Once, I looked up and saw our mother holding her hands over her ears. Later I saw our father standing on the top row of the bleachers, gazing up at the glass-brick windows instead of watching us.

At some point my mother whistled until we both lifted our heads from the water.

"Your lips are blue," she said. "Time to take a break."

"I'm not even cold," I said.

"Susan."

"Fine," I said, hauling myself up on my elbows. "But Julia has to get out too." I accepted the towel she offered me. "Where's Dad?"

"He'll be back in a minute."

Julia climbed out, refused a towel, and sat on the edge of the diving board, swinging her legs.

"Where'd he go?" she said.

Perhaps around the block, though I never bothered to confirm. I joined Julia on the diving board. Our mother rummaged in her purse. When our father returned his jacket was bright with rain, his glasses cloudy. He took them off and held them as if they were stinging his fingertips.

"Now?" our mother said.

Julia grabbed my arm and squeezed it, and I didn't know why. Later, she'd say it was clear that they were about to announce their split. It made no sense to me that I hadn't been able to see it. I was the one, so far, who'd had to explain everything to her, including that she would not get "the kissing disease" after her first game of spin the bottle. (I was the one struck with mononucleosis that year, having kissed no one at all.) It was right in front of me—our father, pacing the top row of bleachers; our mother, clawing at her bag just for something to do with her hands—but I did not see it.

IN COLLEGE, SOMEONE—it might have been Molly—made a joke about the boilerplate divorce talk that '90s parents handed down to their children. It's not your fault. We grew apart. We love you just the same.

My parents were never especially attuned to trends. Perhaps they hadn't heard that part of their job, on the cusp of divorce, was to reassure or protect their children. They approached it much as they did other family-wide tasks—raking up the fallen leaves, clearing the dishes off the dinner table.

In this instance, they asked us how we would like to divide our time. Trish was staying in the house we'd grown up in, at least to start, and our father would rent one half of a duplex in a different part of town. They handed us full ownership of our time, as if we understood time at all.

We knew enough to say that this wasn't the place to make arrangements: not in the lukewarm water of an indoor pool, not dangling your legs off the diving board, not while your father was visibly trying not to cry.

Julia hosted the meeting inside her closet. The light was pink from her lava lamp. A week of anxious gnawing had ruined our fingernails.

We'd been in the same K–12 private school since kindergarten, thanks to the tuition benefits that came with our mother's administrative assistant job. Julia loved *Poetic Justice*, I loved *The Craft*, and we had posters on our respective walls to that effect. Our agreed-upon favorite meal was a sandwich of ham, ketchup, and Tater Tots, preferably on white toast. We both wore more than enough CK One; at school I'd traded a pair of Chuck Taylors that I'd outgrown for a bottle. Even after we owned the CK One, we continued to collect ads for it.

I told her I had a plan: alternating nights.

"What does that even mean?" Julia said.

"It means Monday *Mom*, Tuesday *Dad*, Wednesday *Mom*, Thursday *Dad*."

"Okay," Julia said. "Let's try it."

I AM A mother. I cannot imagine a less convenient arrangement than the one we devised.

Our parents didn't have the energy to resist. They became, in the first months of the divorce, lapsed versions of themselves, and the truth was that I enjoyed it. At both houses we ate in front of the TV. My father had some vague ideas about not wearing miniskirts, but he could be fooled by a long peacoat and dark tights. We had to share a room in his rental, and he decorated it with feathered pink pillows on the twin beds and a purple rag rug; this during a time when I played, nonstop, a Nirvana cassette, when I mourned the end of *My So-Called Life*. Once, I called my mother and asked her to pick me up because Dad was serving turkey sandwiches for dinner, which I hated, I told her, with a "burning passion." She asked if there was anything else to eat, and I acknowledged a container of pasta salad, which I did like, especially when it was made with black olives. *Why don't you try being satisfied with what you have*, my mother said.

Another time, I had a knot in my hair that I couldn't get out, and my father suggested, not unkindly, that he might have to cut it out, and I called my mother, who had never been good at getting knots out of my hair, and who told me to use a brush instead of a comb. This made it worse. Julia got it out eventually. I sat on the floor between her knees, swearing every time she pulled at the root. My father, in a different room, was annoyed with my language, and I was silently annoyed with him.

A PRIVATE CRUELTY, regarding my mother: the origins of her second marriage are still mystifying to me.

In 1997, she was the administrative assistant to the director of development at Lake Tamarack School. In May, she was tasked with arranging a casual lunch for the board of trustees. Glenn Childress, local trusts and estates attorney and newly minted member of the board, offered to give her a ride to the deli to pick up grinders and chips and cookies, an errand that led, a tidy ten months later, to their engagement.

Why? How? She was a perpetually tired, short-tempered woman who complained about the bags under her eyes. She was, at home, a gum chewer and a hair spray devotee. Regarding fashion, she said things like, "I don't really understand clothes." She loved *Three's*

Company. She loved waking early, before the rest of the family was up, and cleaning the already-clean rooms, searching for hidden pockets of dust, sweeping for even one stray crumb. In her house, when you woke up, everything gleamed.

She was practical, punctual, good at the tedious parts of her job, and capable of exuding warmth when it was required. She was—it feels both unkind and factual to say—fairly charmless. She had raised me to think that girls had to dazzle their way into relationships, but I could not imagine her in the act of dazzling.

ONE NIGHT AT Mom's, Julia and I lay on the living-room rug watching *Friends*, each of us with strawberry ice cream that our mother had softened by placing the bowls, briefly, in a pan of hot water. "Wouldn't you rather just live here all the time?" I said. I kept my eyes on the screen as I said it, in case Julia disagreed with me, which she did.

Among her arguments:

Our father would be too lonely.

He had gone through the trouble of putting a room together for us, and it would be too sad to leave our beds sitting there, empty, with those feathered pillows.

We had two parents, who gave of themselves equally. Shouldn't we give them equal time?

Sure, I said. Equality. Yeah.

But I liked our mother's house better, even before she married Glenn, who had discovered that one of the easiest ways to keep her happy was to indulge me. I was a great beneficiary of their relationship. Everything I owned—sunglasses, watch, Discman, backpack—was swiftly upgraded. Glenn and our mother bought and renovated a spacious farmhouse. When they told Julia and me to draw straws for who got the en suite third-floor bedroom, Julia said I could have it, she didn't care.

THE HEATING VENT in Julia's room at Mom and Glenn's stopped working, and the room was too cold to sleep in. Though it took only five days to fix, and there were other rooms she could stay in, that week she brought more and more of her clothing over to Dad's, along with the boy-band poster she'd stolen from a store at the mall on a dare. She enlisted me to hold it taut against the wall while she pushed thumbtacks into its corners.

"I think I just want to live here," she said, smoothing the glossy poster with the back of her hand.

"What?"

She jumped down from the chair she was standing on.

"You heard me." This was one of our father's expressions.

I sat on my side of the room, to which I had added nothing. Her poster shimmered. "You would seriously rather stay here?"

"You'd really rather be at Mom and Glenn's?"

"I like having my own bathroom."

"Uh-huh." She flopped onto her bed and placed her feet against the wall. "You can go live there, then. I'll stay here."

"Well, you can't, like, tell me where to live."

"I'm telling you where *I'm* going to live."

"Okay, okay." I circled the feathered pillow in my arms. "But don't you want to be in the same place as me?"

"Not really."

"Shut up."

"You asked."

"Shut *up*, Julia."

We fought this way often, but it rarely devolved into anything physical. I pulled her hair—an old tactic from when we were much younger children—and she broke free of my hand and laughed at me.

"What is wrong with you?" she said, rubbing the sore spot on her head.

Our father appeared in the doorway. He looked only at Julia as he spoke. He had called our mother, he said, and asked her to take me for the night.

Sledding

January 15, 2001

For Christmas my freshman year of college, my mother and stepfather gave me a cashmere swing coat with silk lining and a Tiffany toggle bracelet engraved with my monogram. I wore both on the night I drove back to school from Massachusetts for the new semester. My mother had told me, not disapprovingly, that I was spoiled, also that I was pretty, and I thought that perhaps this could be my new campus persona: spoiled and pretty. To accentuate this vision, I tied my hair up with a red velvet ribbon and put on lipstick to match.

At the entrance to the Taconic, there were no other cars in the tollbooth line. The stretch of road was familiar to me, and seemingly always overcast, and I was often alone on it, as if everyone but me had been invited to Albany. The man who accepted the coins from my hand whistled at me, and I was flattered—I was not the kind of person who felt bothered or scared by that. I suspected this was not the right response.

In the dorm, there was a note on my whiteboard from Cash—
Come sledding—and I felt the usual thrill of having been invited,
along with reluctance at having to show up alone. There was only
one good sledding hill, and it was a two-mile walk. I pulled my father's Vineyard sweatshirt from my closet and brought it to my nose.
I caught, under my ritual spritz of perfume, a hint of frying oil in the
cotton—I'd last worn it to a twenty-four-hour diner—and I dropped
it into the hamper and set down the lid.

By the time I reached the hill, my face felt burned by the wind.
Tyler, a guy with whom I was vaguely friendly, was known to be an
exuberant drunk; as I approached, he dropped the sled he was holding, picked me up, and spun me around. I shrieked, mostly out of
surprise. My coat swirled as it was meant to. When Tyler set me
down, Cash was looking at me.

"You're late." He grabbed my hem. "What's this?"

"New coat."

"Won't it get ruined?"

"Probably." I ran the back of my hand across the silk lining.
"Maybe I'll just watch."

"No. No watching allowed."

"Shut up," I said. Tyler offered a sip from his beer, and I took it.
Cash dove headfirst onto a sled and vanished. I regretted walking
over; I'd arrived at the party too late. Everyone was already happy,
giddy from beer and malt liquor. Their socks were soaking wet and

they didn't care. It was not the kind of night where I mattered all that much. If I left, in the morning no one would remember that I had been there. Noel Rafferty, who was weeks from dropping out of college altogether, was pulling a sled uphill with two girls on it. "Hey, Zuzu," he said. One of the girls in the sled threw a snowball at him and said, "Mush!"

Molly Pierce had a toboggan that she'd found in her parents' barn over break. "You can't just *stand* there," she said, but when I took a step forward she said, "You're going to ruin your pretty coat." I had a fear, back then, of losing my hard-won reputation as a *really fun person*. I took off my coat and draped it over the branch of a tree.

Molly pulled me onto the toboggan in front of her, wrapping her arms around my rib cage. For a moment I remembered how good it all felt—the stomach drop and helpless scream, the air running up your sleeves and down your neck, the way the snow crunched when you slowed to a stop, how you couldn't see where you were going. Molly and the other girls were messy and carefree—even in the dark I could see they made no effort to maintain their beauty, maybe because they really believed it was there. Mine, I sensed, depended on the angle, on my effort, on what my hair had decided to do. Mine, I felt, needed my protection. Trudging back up the hill, I felt snow melting into my curls, the wind ruining their shape. The ribbon I'd tied them back with had loosened its hold. I was cold and sober, and I wanted to leave.

Cash was by the tree where I'd draped my coat. I wore jeans and a black scoop-neck shirt, with thin cotton socks under my boots. All of it was wet.

"You look freezing, Braeburn," he said.

"I am freezing. I'm heading back."

"Hang on." He unbuttoned his vest. "You can have this."

I thought of how lumpy I'd look in it; all vests had a way of turning my breasts into a bulky ridge.

"No, thanks."

"Just take it."

"I'm fine."

"Come on, I'm being a gentleman, here." He held the vest up by its collar.

"No, thank you."

"I don't get why you bothered to come if you're just going to leave," he said. "At least Tyler got to spin you around first."

I looked at him, but he was staring fixedly at the spot where two sleds had collided. There was riotous, exhilarated laughter, but he and I were silent. To say something so plainly petty, and so possessive, struck me as the equivalent of a confession, and I felt displeasure frilled with something else—with secret, embarrassed happiness. I leaned against him and placed my boots on top of his, which brought our faces much closer.

"What are you doing to me?" he said.

"You're making me taller." I hooked my arms around him. "Didn't you do this, at dances? This is how we danced in middle school."

"You know I never danced at dances."

"Too cool?"

"Obviously."

I leaned closer. His mouth, dry and surprising, rested against my temple.

"Stay here," he said.

"I can't. I'm cold."

"Are you serious?" He tightened his arms around me, but it was only to lift me off him and back onto the ground. He cupped his hands around his mouth and projected his voice across the snow.

"Zuzu's leaving already, everyone," he shouted. "Apparently we're boring her. Apparently she has better things to do."

"Cash," I said.

"Go," he said. "I seriously don't care."

"Well, it seems like you do care a bit."

"You never actually, like, *help* yourself," he said. "You're cold? Get a different coat. Wear a hat or something."

He went to get another beer from where they were buried in the snow. A few people looked at me with what I feared was mild pity.

I lifted my coat off the branch. The silk lining and the cashmere were wet in several places, and there were flakes of bark on one sleeve. Walking the paved path back to the dorms, I expected Cash to run after me.

IN MY ROOM I ate a mug of ramen and went back out to brush my teeth. The hallway was silent. Noel Rafferty was standing at the far end, near the radiator and the windows that let onto the fire escape.

"What are you doing?" I said.

He turned. His hands were in his pockets.

"Waiting for you," he said.

"Ha." I yawned. "I'm getting ready for bed."

"You realize you walk by me all the time like you don't know me."

"Do I?"

"We don't have to be best friends," he said. "But let's not pretend we don't know each other, all right? Because we do."

I didn't deny this. We knew and understood each other well. We were accustomed to dwelling in spaces where nobody thought to look for Black people. At home in western Mass, we referred to ourselves as hicks. He could see a dairy farm from his parents' living-room windows, and I could see a tractor-crossing sign from mine. We'd been raised in old clapboard houses among sugar maples. We were used to our white mothers picking us up from camp or swimming class and our teachers failing to hide their surprise.

"Yeah, okay," I said. I felt sorry for him. He had plenty of friends on campus but he was struggling to keep up. I'd heard he was already on some kind of academic probation.

"We understand each other," he said.

"Sure, Noel." I made a teeth-brushing motion.

"We're pretty much the only mutts around," he said.

I hated that word. I couldn't even stand to repeat it. I told him how much I hated it.

"It's a joke," he said.

"It isn't funny."

"Zuzu, I—"

"We are not *dogs*," I said. "Don't call me a *dog*."

"I didn't call you a *dog*."

"Yes, you *did*," I said. It felt good to dip into the haughty voice that I mostly reserved for my family.

"Well, I'm sorry, then," he said.

"Whatever. I have to brush my teeth."

He stepped forward and held the door open for me.

I LAY IN bed with my clean teeth, thrumming with indignation, my new coat draped over my chair and my boots thrown on the floor, so that when Cash let himself in he almost tripped. He dangled something silver over my upturned face: my bracelet, which he'd found in the snow.

"You lost this," he said.

"Put it on my desk."

He slid my keyboard aside and gently set the bracelet down. I assessed my pajamas—the Vineyard sweatshirt, even though it was dirty, and crushed velvet pants—before I kicked back my blankets and got out of bed to face him.

"James Cashel," I said.

"Susan Braeburn."

I pointed to my answering machine. I had selected and saved

twenty-five messages. Trish's had all been deleted. Glenn's—*Did you know campus security is mailing your parking tickets to the house? Could you settle up, please?*—had also been erased. Julia had called once, presumably drunk, singing "Total Eclipse of the Heart," and I'd kept it so that I could tease her with it later, but the other twenty-four were from Cash. None of them stood out—did I want to get coffee, was I going to the library—but they were all his voice, looking for me.

"What is this?" he said.

"Proof," I said. "You like me, Cash." I kept skipping, one to the next. *Hey Zuzu, it's Cash. Hey Zuzu, it's Cash.*

"This is maybe a little psychotic," he said after the tenth message.

"You're the one who left them."

"You're the one who *saved* them."

"Fine." I reached for the erase button, but he caught my hand.

"Why do you need proof?" he said. "That I like you?"

"On the hill." I needed to wipe my nose. "What did you call me? Incapable?"

"I never said that."

"You said I never help myself."

"I just didn't want you to be cold."

"Next time you think I'm cold, you can bring me a cup of tea."

"Okay, okay." We stood there in silence for nearly a minute. "We need to get some sleep," he said.

He did not mean that we should lie side by side. When he returned to my room it was morning—after seven, at least, because that's when the campus café opened, and that's where he'd bought the take-out cup of tea that he had left, precariously, on top of my clock radio.

THAT BRACELET HAD long been property of Agnes Blair, who kept it on our dresser in a small ceramic dish. She'd worn it often when we started dating, and even when she no longer liked the way it looked, she said she liked having it around.

Really Fun Person

October 15, 2001

C ash and I lived on the same floor of the vegetarian house our sophomore year, though we did not share a wall. A summerlong separation had made us shy at first, but we signed up for dish and cooking duty together through most of the fall. I was salting a pot of water when he came up behind me and covered my eyes with his hands.

"Guess who," he said.

"We're the only people here."

"Are we?"

"Blake's at his girlfriend's, Alex is at the gym, and Molly took the train into the city."

"We're alone?"

"Until Alex gets back, yes."

"Then why are we wasting time in here?"

I switched the knob to *off* and turned to face him. He looked up at the ceiling, put his hands behind his back, cracked his knuckles.

"Help me with the trash, would you?" he said.

I followed him out the back door, down the rotting wooden steps, to the row of metal bins. A recent storm had knocked some of the shingles off the roof, and I kicked one into a pile of wet leaves. Cash dropped the bags into the bin and slid the raccoon-deterrent cords into place, and I kicked another shingle and looked up at my window. Through a gap in the blinds I could see the fire-colored tapestry I had pinned to the wall.

"Since when do you like *this* stuff?" my mother had asked when she moved me in. She wasn't wrong. I was spoiled and pretty, I wore silver and ribbons; the ratty Vineyard sweatshirt was a marked departure from my usual polished coordination. I was a vegetarian mostly because the only thing I knew how to make was pasta and salad in a bag with bottled dressing. But Cash had insisted, in sporadic emails over the summer, that I make a bid for the empty room on the second floor, and I had done it, and now it was mine.

"What 'help' did you need me for, exactly?" I said as we walked back to the house.

"Your very presence helps me, Zuzu."

He held the door open for me and gestured that I should go first. At the sink, we washed our hands under the same stream of water.

"Tofu or tempeh?" he said.

"I hate tempeh."

He opened the fridge and said, "I have bad news for you, darling."

He crumbled the tempeh into a pan of onions and garlic. I sat at the small kitchen table, where none of us actually ate because it held a massive CD player and two shoeboxes full of CDs. I was digging through the box, looking for something I thought he'd like, when the front door banged open.

"Thank God," Molly said, dropping her bags on the floor. "I am so fucking hungry." She took a banana from the counter and peeled it. "There were like fifteen hockey teams on the train. It was horrible."

"Poor Molly Pierce had to take public transportation," Cash said from the stove.

"Shut up." She glanced at me, then at the CD player. "Zuzu, don't you think it's too quiet in here?"

She leaned over, pulled out Bob Dylan's *Desire*, selected "Hurricane," and sang along, grabbing a set of take-out chopsticks and drumming them everywhere: on the counter, on top of my head, and then, for half a minute, on each of Cash's shoulders, until he reached behind him without looking and grabbed her wrists in one hand. She screamed. He turned and picked her up, dripping oil from his wooden spoon onto the floor. Her hair—like mine, voluminous curls, although hers were blond and there was a floppy elasticity to them—swung down his back because her head was over his shoulder. The chopsticks were briefly airborne, then fell at my feet. I couldn't look at either of them. The music was loud, the skillet was starting to smoke. Molly, not I, was the really fun person.

"Why don't you two just go upstairs," I said. Neither of them heard me.

I went upstairs. I would like to say that in my room I simply turned to one of my interests—that I read one of the nineteenth-century novels I'd been assigned in my English seminar, or that I called another friend and left the house. I had a car, parked right next to Cash's Jeep; in two hours I could have been soaking in my tub at Mom and Glenn's. Instead I stared in the mirror, pinched my sides, fluffed my hair at the roots, then tried to smooth it back down. It occurred to me, not for the first time, that although I was indeed pretty—I heard it every day—I was not pretty enough, or not the right kind of pretty. It was a thought that repulsed me with its cruelty and its little knot of fear. It was a thought I would have denied having, no matter who asked. I did not think I could bear it if living in that drafty, inconvenient house meant I had to witness Cash and Molly locked in some kind of romantic dance. There was always a wait list of disappointed vegetarians; I could swap rooms with someone in a dorm in a matter of hours. I resolved to do it, opening my suitcases and filling them with clothes that were still on their hangers. I climbed on my bed—a double mattress on casters—and pulled a corner of the tapestry down.

"Knock, knock," Cash said, letting himself in. He was holding a bowl of polenta, with a thin orange sauce of olives and sun-dried tomatoes on it. He held it out, an offering. "I'm saving you from the tempeh."

"Oh."

"What are you doing?" He set the bowl on my desk. "Did it fall?"

I shook my head.

He knelt down by my suitcase. "Are you going somewhere?"

"Actually." I sat. The tapestry dangled. "I'm not sure if I want to stay here."

"Ha."

"I'm serious."

"Is it this?" He held up the bowl again. "You don't like this either?"

I took a large, demonstrative bite, burning the roof of my mouth, and then he took a bite, using my fork.

"It's not that bad, is it?" he said.

"It's good."

He was watching me, waiting for me to explain myself. I could not tell him the truth. I looked up at the tapestry.

"I'm kind of bored here," I said.

He nodded slowly—a habit of his when he was displeased—and then he stood up and motioned for me to follow him.

"Let me show you one thing," he said.

His room had the requisite tapestry (green and blue) and a futon with plaid sheets. He read at least one newspaper a day, a section at a time, so that his floor was never clear of their pages. Molly said that it looked as if he were always house-training a puppy.

"You know how those branches fell off the tree in the storm," he said, pushing open a window. "It turns out now I have unimpeded roof access."

I had to crawl over his desk to follow him onto the porch roof. The shingles were wet, littered with small twigs and plastered with leaves. We sat hip-to-hip, each of us hugging our knees. It was a dead-end street with a few other college-owned buildings on it, including Health Services, a concrete cube with posters in the windows advocating safe sex. On the corner, there was a restaurant beloved for its garlic knots and its failure to card. The air smelled of recent rain and garlic and dryer sheets and beer. I was wearing my Vineyard sweatshirt, and I pulled my hands all the way inside the sleeves. Across the street, a football game brightened someone else's TV.

"What's going on with you and Molly?" I said.

"Nothing."

"Would you even tell me if there was?"

"Would you really want to know?"

"Oh, my God. You can't ever just answer a question, can you."

"Jesus, you're cranky," he said. "I made you dinner."

"I know."

"If you move out, you think anybody will make you dinner?"

"Probably not."

"Definitely not," he said.

I could feel the warmth, the slightly beseeching tone, the polenta and olives, the *darling*, start to recede. His other mode was taciturn, almost comical in its gruffness. Below us, Molly or Alex had turned up the music in the kitchen: "Hurricane" again. Another car drove by, and I saw people looking up at us, and I wondered if, through a pane of glass, at roughly thirty miles an hour, there was any way to mistake us for a couple.

Gazebo

⁓

August–September 2012

When Agnes and I first moved out of the city, I took a walk to the riverside park on a Tuesday night with Gideon strapped to my chest. We passed a couple in the gazebo—the woman with her legs thrown across the man's lap, their baby in a bassinet stroller parked several feet away. They were laughing, and there was a bottle of wine between them and wax paper from the deli on Main Street. I was close enough to see that one of them didn't eat their sandwich crusts. She was slapping his arm with a muslin cloth, and I heard her warn him not to wake the baby, and I walked out of the park and stopped to send myself a text—just the word "gazebo," but I knew what it meant. It meant: You have a family, and you deserve happiness, and you have to try.

I went back the following week with Gideon in the stroller. In the storage space beneath his seat I packed a soft blanket, a travel mug full of Chardonnay, an open jar of green olives, and a stale half of a baguette. It was a sorrowful picnic, but as I gathered the items in the kitchen I'd felt the warm spread of anticipation on my chest and back, as if I were going on a date. I set Gideon on the striped blanket and let him gnaw on a chunk of baguette. I wished that someone were coming to meet us, someone who would find me beautiful, would remark on how good a mother I was, as they walked to us across the grass.

In fact, sometimes Agnes did say those things—both that I was a good mother, and that I was beautiful. The truth was that I wanted to hear it on the hour. The truth was that I wanted some expression of gratitude every single time I did something to care for her or our son. I felt drained by each task. Furthermore—certainly my mother had implied this about herself—I felt that all the labor put my beauty at risk. Beauty could be worked away, could be worked out of you. Down the sink, every time I washed a dish. Into the washer, into the dryer, under the vacuum, out with the diapers, stuck in the board books, spoiled as spit-up milk.

IN THE CHILDREN'S section of the library, I saw a hot-pink flyer announcing a parents' group that met weekly in the park. I already walked to the gazebo on a regular basis, out of restlessness; now I had purpose. I told Agnes that I was "invited to join a moms' group." This pleased her, as I knew it would, because it meant I was getting to know people in our town, and she didn't want me to be lonely.

She was less pleased as the weeks passed. The group—out of six women, I was the only one with a wife—was giving me ideas. Most of the mothers had negotiated for a weekend morning off. Their husbands took the baby with them to do the week's grocery shopping, for instance, while the wives slept in.

Agnes told me that would be impossible for her.

Two of the women in the group were lawyers on parental leave, and two of them were married to lawyers, and it seemed to me that it wasn't technically *impossible* for Agnes to let me sleep in on Sunday mornings. What was impossible was to convince her otherwise.

When I spoke to the group, I didn't mention having gone to law school—I didn't want to tell them that I had failed the bar two times. In fact, I didn't speak much at all. I didn't want to betray Agnes by complaining about her in front of other women, implicitly or otherwise. Sometimes, watching my son crawl around by the gazebo, I remembered that I'd done it, my success was right in front of me. The snacks we all shared were organic, the sun was warm, there wasn't a piece of litter in sight. It was a Hudson Valley town with rainbow-flag stickers in the shop windows. This was the adulthood I'd dreamed about, the kind my friend Claire had observed as a child, the kind she called "boring" and said she wanted to avoid: immaculate houses, each in quiet competition with its neighbor, T-ball and swim lessons, and holiday cards. Every bit of this had always sounded glorious to me. I didn't care if my clothes were the same as everyone else's clothes. I'd stood out plenty enough already in my life, and I was fine to fall into place if the place would take me.

I joined in the light marriage chatter—anniversary gifts, vacation plans—but a polite wall descended when we strayed into deeper territory. Eventually, I understood that my intimate life could not be mined for humor, or for empathy; it could not be included, really. They didn't know how to approach it, and neither did I. At that point, Agnes and I coexisted in exhausted silence that had no space for, or hint of, desire. This felt like a different kind of confession, one that contained more sadness to it than could be tolerated while we sat there and talked about preschool waitlists.

Occasionally, the other moms complained about the mistakes their husbands made: forgetting the sunscreen, adding sugar to applesauce, letting the children nap past five. The closest I came to joining those conversations was to tell everyone about our storage unit in Jersey City. My across-the-street neighbor, Jane Lytton, was particularly amused by the fact that we could no longer even recall what we were paying for, other than my dearly missed Vineyard sweatshirt. "I think there are chili pepper lights in there? Maybe a lava lamp?" I'd said once, to her great delight.

Storage unit aside, Jane always assumed the best of Agnes.

"I mean, I doubt she just walks by a sink full of dishes," Jane said. "I doubt she walks by an overflowing trash can and turns on the TV."

But she did! Agnes walked by dishes and trash cans all the time. Sometimes when she got home around ten she'd fry herself an egg and then leave the skillet on the stove, and if I decided not to wash it for her, it would sit there for days. Days. By the time I washed it, the anger I felt didn't even make sense: It had taken me two minutes, it was just a frying pan. Think of the money she made for our family in two minutes at her desk.

THE LAST TIME I went to the group meeting by the gazebo, we talked about where we'd grown up. Some of them knew Ashworth, my hometown, because they'd visited one of the area colleges. It's so beautiful there, they said.

But so far away from everything.

I agreed.

Gideon was chewing a yogurt-dipped pretzel. I pulled him into my lap, inhaled the scent of his scant hair. I told them I'd wanted to live in this town since I first came to visit. When they asked if it was everything I'd hoped for, I said yes, of course.

When the group ended for the day, it occurred to me that I had never tried to find Claire's house, the house of Pernod and walnuts, stained glass and cleaning lady, father who got his shoes polished while he waited for the train. I knew it was on the same street as the town's famed historic house because Claire had pointed it out to me. The tours, she'd said, were excruciating, but it was a rite of passage if you'd grown up on the street.

I looked it up on my phone. Claire's street was closer to mine than I'd realized. After dinner I bundled Gideon back into his stroller, gave him a pouch of pureed prunes, and walked east on Carmel Lane, crossed Main Street and passed the gazebo, walked two more blocks, took a right on Hearthstone, then a left on Highland. The museum was closed, but electric candles burned in the mullioned windows. Even though I knew nobody lived there, the warm light almost convinced me that there were people behind those windows, living contentedly.

The rest of the houses on the street were tucked behind gates or high hedges, and none of them looked familiar to me. I remembered standing in Claire's mudroom—there was a row of hooks, and I'd chosen one for my coat—but not how it had looked from the outside. I walked to the end of the street and turned around. I walked the opposite length of it, until I was standing across the way from the museum, where the light still tricked me, where I felt I could almost hear people laughing inside.

My son kicked in the stroller and pushed his prunes away.

"We can go home in one second," I told him. "It's just that I know it's here. I *know* it's right around here."

I couldn't find it. I searched for the address using Claire's full name, but nothing came up. Gideon started to cry, and instead of taking him home I jogged him around the block, hoping the speed would calm him, but he cried harder, and I still had no idea which of the houses was the one in which I'd spent a hopeful night.

"Sorry, G," I said, turning back toward Main Street. It was past time for his bath. He threw his pouch of prunes, and in the seconds before I picked it up it oozed a dark, sweet puddle onto the sidewalk.

Invitations

November 2001

I was often in Cash's room when his mother called. Sometimes he put her on speaker and told her to say hello, so that over time one of the first things Bronwen Cashel asked was, "Is Zuzu there?" She then addressed her questions to me: Was her son keeping up with his laundry? (Yes.) Was he studying? (Yes.) Drinking? (Thursday through Sunday, pretty much.) Driving at the same time? (Never.)

"I like having my spy there in the house with you, James," Bronwen said.

"She's not your spy," Cash said. "She's on my side."

OUT OF DUTY, the Cashels were spending Thanksgiving at an assisted-living facility in Connecticut—not a grandparent, Cash said, but a great-aunt he had met only twice. When Bronwen called, her son was foam rolling after the gym. I was sitting on his desk, drinking coffee and looking longingly at the porch roof, whitened by the season's first snow.

"I need to tell Aunt Portia whether or not you're joining us," Bronwen said. "As a *courtesy*, I need to tell her. I don't expect her to remember."

Cash looked at me. He seemed to be speaking to me, and not to his mother, when he asked if skipping it were unforgivable.

"No, not unforgivable," Bronwen said. "You could stand to send some flowers though." She paused. "Is my spy there?"

"I'm here," I said.

"And what are your holiday plans?"

"Going to my mother's," I said. Cash was putting the foam roller away, changing out of a sweaty T-shirt and into a fresh one.

"Do me a favor and take him in, would you?" Bronwen said. "If you have room at the table? Otherwise he'll sit in that empty house and eat cereal."

"Mom." Cash was laughing. "You can't invite me to somebody else's Thanksgiving."

BRONWEN COULD. BRONWEN did. As a token of thanks, she sent my mother a massive cornucopia that became the dinner centerpiece. She also sent a gift basket from a famous gourmet shop: preserved lemons, cherry compote, mint jelly, tomato jam. My mother lined the jars up on a countertop and refused to let anyone touch them, as if she couldn't have bought them herself.

OCCASIONALLY, I COUNSEL myself against this particular set of memories: They are too idyllic, it could not have been as I recall it. It was true that Cash and I were at our best when it was just the two of us, with no friends to impress or dissuade, with no Molly Pierce. Did we really rest our hands together, one on top of the other, not entwined but *together*, on the shift stick as I drove us through the Berkshires and back to Ashworth? We did. We just pretended we didn't.

MY ERRATIC VEGETARIAN habits were ignored at home, but for Cash the fridge was packed with greens, and Glenn picked up a mushroom potpie from the deli. My mother was plainly delighted by how good-looking Cash was, and after her first whiskey sour she referred to him mostly as "you handsome thing." He found her funny. He was unflaggingly polite. When he started to clear the table after dinner, Trish told him to sit, but he said he hadn't been raised to be waited on. He rinsed the plates, and I loaded them into the dishwasher while my mother and Glenn went to the garage for the Christmas ornaments—it was our tradition to get the tree the Friday after Thanksgiving—and as soon as we heard the door slam behind them, Cash kissed my forehead, and I tilted my face so quickly that he kissed my mouth. He tasted like rosemary and sage and olive oil and wine. I was holding a serving fork. He still held, under the running water, the cut-glass dish clotted with cranberry sauce.

There had been no question regarding where he would sleep. Glenn brought his bags to the downstairs guest room, which, while clean, was also a kind of repository for things my family no longer wanted. This had to do with habit, not moral code; if anything, I was insulted by the assumption that Cash and I didn't share a bed. I could not make the words *You can sleep with me upstairs* come out; instead of saying this, I waited for him to sense the invitation, to hear it through my closed mouth, to see it in my face, to wait until all the lights were doused, to float up on silent feet. This did not happen, though I woke throughout the night and swept my hand across the empty side of the bed, as if I might find him there.

In the morning, I discovered that Cash was clearing the snow from the roof and windows of each car in the driveway. His face was mottled and he kept wiping his nose with his sleeve. Snow melted in his hair as he worked.

"He's a keeper," my mother said, pouring coffee into a mug.

"Not mine to keep."

"Bring this out to him."

"No way. This one's for me."

My mother made a disapproving sound in her throat.

I went outside with my coat unzipped over a sweatshirt and yoga pants. Cash was blowing on his hands.

"You could have borrowed gloves," I said.

"Nah. I'm almost done."

"My mom is looking at you like you're the northern lights, by the way."

"I am the northern lights, more or less." He lowered the thick-bristled snow brush to the ground and swept a little toward my untied boots, causing me to shriek and back away; then he turned and waved at Trish, who stood at the kitchen's French doors.

I had more access than I wanted, at that moment, to my mother's mind. I could see myself from where she stood, the daughter who needed to stand up straight and trim her split ends more often, the one who had managed to bring home this boy but didn't know what to do next. *This is what it could be like*, she was probably thinking. *This is what she could have.*

THAT WAS THE only time Cash came to Thanksgiving, but it was not the only time I brought a guest. I invited Agnes to come home with me for Thanksgiving our first year of law school, when we were still just friends. As I recall, she fell asleep in my room while we were watching *Sex and the City*. I thought nothing of it, my friend taking up more than her fair share of the bed. My mother said of Agnes, *Well, she certainly seems bright*, which was not, in that house, much of a compliment.

Chandelier

August 2008

When I told Agnes that Cash would be in town, we were carrying a velvet love seat up the stairs of our new place on Fourteenth Street, a week before orientation at the law school. A dog barked incessantly somewhere in the building, and someone had spilled cherry pie filling all over the floor of the trash room. There was an empty pickle jar in the middle of the hall, and Agnes kicked it and watched it roll away.

"Maybe we chose the wrong place." Her green bandanna was no longer neatly tied around her head, and where it had been pushed up, her reddish-blond hair curled with sweat. "Why would I say yes to a Murphy bed?"

"I'll take the Murphy bed."

"I need a break." She lowered her side of the love seat down to the floor, but I continued to hold mine.

"So my friend Cash might stop by this week," I said.

She swatted the love seat. "I'm worried this fucker won't fit through the door."

It fit. It fit, and even though there were bars over our windows, we looked into a small courtyard with a dry fountain, which felt elegant. Our galley kitchen had a sink too small to wash Agnes's wooden salad bowl. The finest feature was a closet wallpapered in yellow roses and lit, improbably, by a small chandelier.

"If you go across the street to get cold noodles," Agnes said, "I'll give you a million dollars."

"I expect the first installment next week."

"No problem," Agnes said.

I got up, opening a box full of towels to wipe the sweat under my breasts, unearthing among the towels an old LSAT study guide. Studying for the LSAT had proved to me that I could endure incredible tedium; that I could be bored and get through it. I had never found within myself, as so many of my friends had, the will to keep running even though it hurt. I could not meditate—I had tried, and I had failed, unless meditation meant cataloging your social mistakes in silence. This, though, I could do: feel bored, stick with it, and get the answer right. Glenn was delighted by my admission to law school and by the prospect that he wouldn't have to support me until I was fifty-five (a direct quote). Having gladly accepted both the tuition and living expenses from Glenn, I was now confronted with the possibility that I had no interest, whatsoever, in practicing law.

"Do I even want to be a lawyer, though?" I said, refolding the towel.

"You've come this far." Agnes stretched all the way across the love seat. "I'm starving, hint hint."

I went across the street for the noodles, and when I turned from the counter with our order I saw that Agnes was standing on the sidewalk. She wore loose shorts, a white polo shirt, and the bandanna. She looked young and full of adrenaline, as if she were just home from after-school sports.

"Why are you down here?" I said. "Is this about the million dollars? Are you going to renege?"

She shook her head and took the bag from me. "Let's eat these and then go do something," she said.

I was starting to enjoy her version of impulsivity, even though sometimes her "Let's do something" meant signing into a special collections room at a library to look at a set of letters between two scholars I'd never heard of. Another time, she had found us last-minute tickets to a musical so strident that I kept making excuses to leave the theater, until finally I sat in the lobby and drank root beer and read a magazine someone had dropped on the floor. When she came out to find me during the first standing ovation, she laughed and said, "Okay, I guess you hated that."

We ate the noodles while we walked, and then we stopped outside a gallery opening that neither of us felt dressed to navigate. It was enough to hear the happy crowd inside, and to catch glimpses of their good clothes, and to have our hands touch, accidentally or not, as we stood side by side.

On the walk back to our apartment, we stopped at a gelato shop.

A man in an apron was mopping the floor. The door was still propped open, and he addressed us without looking up.

"We're closing for the night." He stopped mopping and turned in the direction of the metal canisters. "There's a little mint left. You can have it for free if you want."

"Mint's my favorite anyway," Agnes said.

He set the mop aside, went behind the counter, scraped the last bit of bright-green gelato into a cup, then dropped the cup in a bag and tossed it to Agnes—"Don't walk on my floor," he said—and as she caught it, we both looked up and saw the same chandelier that glowed weakly in our closet.

"It's a sign," Agnes said, offering me a tiny wooden spoon.

"Sign of what?"

"No idea. But it's a sign."

I made fun of her throughout the week, referring to random objects as "signs," but both of us fell silent the next time we passed the gelato shop and found that the only light fixture hanging from the ceiling was a rectangle of frosted glass. We agreed that it was possible we had conjured the chandelier. It seemed increasingly possible that our world was primarily comprised of our own shared thoughts and impressions, and that we expanded it, when necessary, to acknowledge we were not alone.

Agatha

September 1, 2008

In preparation for Cash's visit I bought farmers market carrots with the tops attached, a carton of golden raspberries, a loaf of seeded bread, and a gorgeous chunk of honeycomb. Of course he ate none of it. I just liked the feeling of shopping for him.

He arrived, freshly hired at a bank in Boston, a little embarrassed by his new haircut.

He asked if we had any beer. When Agnes said no, he looked at me as if she'd kicked him in the shins.

"You're telling me Zuzu Braeburn doesn't have a six-pack in her fridge?"

"Unfortunate but true," I said.

"What happened to you, darling?" he said.

I shrugged.

He was sitting on the futon, and I was standing across the room with my back against the wall. Agnes was at the window, first adjusting the fan, then just watching us. The sun came right through her gauzy dress, and the fan played with the ends of her hair. I wanted her to leave us alone, but I didn't know how to tell her.

"We're going to go out," I said. "So if you want to come . . ."

"I can't," she said.

I tried to feign disappointment, but as soon as Cash and I were out in the hall we started to run, which felt both mean and exhilarating. I would have liked to keep running with him.

We found a bar on University Place with giant ceiling fans, and we ordered ice wine and tamari almonds. I could tell from the way we were sitting that nothing was going to happen. He braced his legs far away from mine underneath the table. The bar played a mix of New Order and Roxy Music.

"This wine is sweet," he said. "Maybe too sweet?"

"Want something else?"

"Nah." He flipped the menu over and back again, then took an almond from the bowl and bit into it. "These were sixteen dollars," he said. "What do you think, a dollar a nut?"

"I don't know, Cash. I guess."

He spun the stem of his glass between two fingers.

"Heard from Molly?" I said.

"Yeah. She's running around Barcelona."

"Doing what?"

"Getting ready to run around another city, probably." He released the glass. "I don't think I like your roommate."

"Maybe *she* doesn't like *you*."

"Everyone likes me." He dragged his finger through the salt in the bowl.

I made the mistake, then, of trying to describe Agnes in earnest. She was the kind of friend who made you Jell-O when you had a summer cold, if you were a person who found Jell-O soothing (I was). She would proofread your law school application essay before she had finished her own. She had recently wandered into my room with a bottle of nail polish, propped a foot on the edge of my bed, and painted her toenails a rosy orange. We did not speak at all—I had music on—and I found myself admiring the bones of her ankles, and the occasional bolt of red in her mostly blond hair.

"Is the light better in here, or something?" I said when she'd finished.

"Not really." She tightened the cap on the bottle. "I just like being around you."

I waited for her to backpedal. There was no gentle shove, no mild insult to undermine what she'd said. No joke to pretend she didn't mean it. She did mean it.

"Why are we talking about this girl?" Cash said.

"I'm just saying, it's not personal. She's awkward with everyone at first."

"I seriously don't care."

"Well, sorry to bore you."

"You should be."

I finished my drink. "What do *you* want to talk about, then?"

"Not Agatha."

"*Agnes.*"

"Tomato, to-mah-to," he said.

He paid for the almonds and ice wine, and then we went to Diesel in Union Square, where one of our friends worked, but it wasn't her shift. On our way out, a guy on a bike almost ran into me. Cash threw his arm in front of my chest, the way my mother used to do when she slammed on the brakes in the car. Ordinarily, this would have resulted in him crowing that he was a hero, that I owed him everything, and it would have become one of our stupid inside jokes, but I didn't want to joke around with him. His hostility toward Agnes was bothering me.

We walked a few blocks without talking, then stopped at a bodega for a six-pack, which he bought. When we crossed Fourteenth Street against the light, he asked if I'd be his lawyer in the event of a jaywalking ticket.

"Maybe," I said. "You seem like you'd be a fairly uncooperative client."

"You know I'd be the best client you ever had." He was holding the bag from the bodega out to me. I took it.

"You're not coming up?"

"Don't think so. Maybe next time we should hang out alone?"

"We are alone."

He nodded at my apartment building.

"This is not alone," he said.

"Why don't you marry me. Then we'd be alone all the time."

"Dammit." He snapped his fingers. "I forgot the ring."

"Ha."

He reached for my hand, swung it between us, and dropped it.

"It would have to be huge," he said.

"What?"

"Your ring."

"That's true. You wouldn't want to disappoint me."

"Never," he said. He was already walking toward the subway. Before he went down the staircase he blew me a kiss.

AGNES WAS RUNNING water into the sink when I unlocked the door. She had changed into red mesh shorts and a white undershirt, and the room smelled of burned popcorn and a cinnamon candle. She had been raised to believe that walking around barefoot ruined the soles of your feet. Even though it was a hot night, she wore ribbed red-and-green socks her parents had given her for Christmas. Her calves bulged with muscle. She wore her thick hair parted in the center and curved toward her chin, as if it wanted to cup her face and protect her.

"What happened to your buddy?" she said.

"He wanted to stay out, I guess."

"I thought you guys might get a hotel room or something."

"It's not that kind of thing."

"Kind of seemed like it was."

"A little bit," I said. "But that was a long time ago. We're really just friends."

"Looks like you're stuck with me, then."

She flopped onto the love seat. Her parents had not yet given her the massive grandfather clock that would effectively block the love seat. We did not yet think of our belongings as "ours." I sat next to her and she draped her legs over mine.

"Zuzu," she said.

I bent forward and kissed her knee, and then her other knee, and then she said, "Wait, wait, wait, I don't think I can handle this yet." I told her, truthfully, that I wasn't even sure why I'd done it.

"Oh, I know why you did it," she said.

BRUSHING MY TEETH, I worried that bringing my lips to her knees had ruptured our friendship, that in the morning I would be too embarrassed to look at her, and that it would soon be evident that one of us needed to move out. Instead, in the morning, we made coffee and talked about what you should wear on your first day of law school, and there was no aftermath, and no shame.

Little Berries

When she finished making pancakes, Agnes suggested a family walk. Gideon led the way, wearing a whistle he'd dug out of the emergency kit I kept in the trunk of the car. He gave it a short blast at every crosswalk. Ten minutes in, Agnes told us to go ahead, that she had work emails to tend to, that she'd catch up when she could. Gideon and I stopped at the library so he could run up the staircase and slide down the metal handrail. When he tired of that, we crossed the street to the riverside park and its weather-battered gazebo. Agnes joined us there, and we watched Gideon chop at the air with two long sticks.

"Look how easily he entertains himself," Agnes said.

"Yeah."

"I give you the credit," she said.

I wasn't sure what she meant, but I knew she was trying to give me a compliment. I stepped closer to her. We studied our son, hands in our pockets, shivering. It would have felt strange and performative to kiss her—we had long ago lost the way to a casual kiss—but I felt an urge to show affection, and I rested my head on her shoulder.

"How's work," I said.

"Interminable."

"But you love it."

"I do."

Gideon approached us with what I mistook, at first, for a sprig of flowers, but was in fact a small branch with clusters of dark berries.

"Where'd you get those little berries?" I said.

"From my pocket."

"Before you put them in your pocket?"

"On a bush next to the library." He held the berries above his open mouth.

"Don't," I said, grabbing the branch from him. He made the same disgruntled hiss he made when I turned off the TV.

"Could you maybe calm down, Zuzu," Agnes said.

The berries were purple-black and shiny, with a wrinkly texture. When I sniffed them I smelled licorice but also the slightly singed odor of a freshly vacuumed room.

"Do you even know what these are?" I said.

"Yes," Agnes said. "They're berries."

I turned the branch in my hand.

"I've never seen them before."

"Here, let me . . ." She pulled her phone from her pocket and took a photo.

"Are you looking them up?" I said.

"Hang on." She was still typing, a smile on her face. "Okay. All good. I sent the picture to Heidi, and she says they're fine to eat."

Gideon looked back and forth between us. He had a fine scar on his nose from a fall the first time he went ice-skating.

"I don't care what Heidi says. I don't think we should be eating random berries from a bush outside a library."

"Give them back, Mom," he said.

"Not if you're going to eat them."

"But I'm *hungry*."

"Here." I pulled a package of flatbread crackers from my bag, and he tore them open as he walked away.

"I told you they were fine," Agnes said.

"He's happy with his crackers."

"That's not the point." She pressed on a splintered floorboard in the gazebo.

"What are these berries called?" I said. "Have you ever had one?"

"I'll eat one right now."

I dropped the branch onto the floor and slid my foot over the fruit, crushing it.

"Unbelievable."

"What if Heidi mistook those berries for something else? What if the photo wasn't clear?"

"The photo was clear." Agnes took her pot of lip balm from her pocket and used her pinkie to slide a layer over her mouth.

"Why is it so important to you that our son eat some random berries?"

"Why," she said, tossing the lip balm from hand to hand, "do you think you get to sign off on all of my decisions?"

"I don't—"

"You don't trust me," she said. "I don't get to make a move without Zuzu's official stamp of approval."

I was tempted to name a recent decision she'd made without my approval. She'd ordered an expensive cherry rocking chair for a narrow corner of our kitchen, even though I'd told her it wouldn't fit. It banged the wall every time someone sat in it, scraping the paint.

I was tempted to say this, but we'd already fought about the chair, both when she bought it and when it arrived.

I was tempted to run away from the gazebo, to kick off my shoes, to push through the reedy vegetation at the river's edge, to jump in with my clothes on, to taste the dirty water, to feel my limbs grow sore while I swam an inexact, sloppy freestyle, until when I turned for a breath I no longer recognized the trees.

Instead, as we cut back up the hill and onto Main Street, she told me she had to run an errand and that she'd meet us back at the house. I watched her walk away between a tunnel of light-adorned trees, past one shop after another, all of them overpriced, all of them closed. What errand? It was a Sunday evening, deep blue, loneliness easy. Even our house—cream clapboard and green shutters, dormer windows on the third floor, glass sidelights flanking the heavy front door—looked lonely to me.

Gideon and I let ourselves in through the garage, placing our shoes on a rack by the door, something Agnes was usually "too tired" to do. He opened a bottle of limeade and poured two glasses, and although the drink was too sweet for me, I loved his gesture too much to decline it. I sipped the limeade and scrolled on my phone. Cash hadn't written back to my previous message. I wrote, Do you like limeade and erased it. I wrote, Would you let Portia eat mystery berries and erased that too. I wrote, What will we do when I come to visit?, inviting the stupid response I received, a GIF of older women in a water aerobics class.

Laundry

December 4, 2009

We got married before we'd even kissed.

This was how I sometimes thought about Agnes. There was so much about her I already knew. She set a two-minute timer each time she brushed her teeth. She cleaned her wallet at night, in bed, and stacked her loose change on the nightstand. She saved rubber bands—if she bought a pint of blueberries, and the cashier snapped a band around the container, she kept the band, believing she could make use of it.

We took turns dropping off and picking up the household laundry at a wash-and-fold on Third Avenue. Bringing the fragrant, plastic-wrapped bundle home to her, I felt that I bore a magnificent gift. She was always so happy to see her clothes. I stopped telling her when I was going to pick it up because I loved the look of surprised joy on her face. I believed the look was a little bit about the laundry, and mostly about me.

Trouble

I n the hours before Julia called to tell me about our father, Gideon
and I ate ziti with butter in front of the TV while Agnes, who
had a cold and was working from home, stayed in her office upstairs. It was Thursday, and my wife had spoken to me fewer than
ten times since I crushed berries beneath my heel in the gazebo. She
had spoken once to accuse me of breaking a fridge magnet, once to
ask me to write a check for the utility bill, and once, as I was writing
the check, to tell me not to make frequent use of her good fountain
pen. Every time I'd shouted up the stairs to offer her tea or a sandwich, she'd opened her office door just to say no.

Roughly thirty minutes before Julia called, after Gideon went to
bed, I texted Cash.

> ZUZU: I'm in trouble with A, as usual
>
> CASH: what'd you do
>
> ZUZU: I don't know
>
> ZUZU: I am generally disappointing I think
>
> CASH: not to me

The Rupture

December 9, 2002

The first time my eardrum ruptured my junior year, I didn't know what it was. The slowly building pressure burst as I crossed the quad. At the campus infirmary I received a prescription for antibiotics, foaming ear drops, and something for the pain. It hurt too much to drive, and I called Cash from one of the nurse's phones and asked him to pick me up. Waiting for him on the sidewalk, I beheld our old home, the vegetarian house, across the street. The shingled face hid behind a network of construction material. The school had concluded that it was too dangerous to allow students to live there until, among other items, the roof had been repaired. Molly lived off campus, but Cash and I had both retreated to the dorms.

In his Jeep, on the way to the pharmacy, Cash reached across me to open the glove box, wadded up a napkin, and held it against my ear, steering with his left hand.

"What are you doing?" I said.

"It's dripping."

The only other people I could think of who might have done that for me were my mother or sister. *He loves me*, I thought. *Really, he does.*

He might have loved me, but he was about to leave for several months abroad, a fact I was still struggling to absorb.

"When you're in London, who's going to handle my assorted emergencies?" I said. "What if my appendix bursts?"

"Your appendix will not burst between January and March, I can assure you."

"What if it does?"

He made a clucking sound.

"I'm not your only friend."

"You kind of are, though," I said.

At the counter, the pharmacist didn't ask if I was on the pill, but he was emphatic that my medications would compromise the pill's efficacy. "You've *got* to use a backup method while you're on these," he said, gesturing at the condom display.

"Okay," I said.

"Tell him it's not optional." The pharmacist nodded at Cash, who was looking at water bottles.

"Okay. I'll tell him."

"Tell me what?" Cash said, glancing up.

"It can wait," I said, knowing he would forget to ask.

There were sheets of stick-on earrings near the register, and I bought them. I wanted to cover my body in tiny little hearts. I wanted to cover Cash's body in tiny little hearts. I was grateful to my ear, despite the horrible burn.

THE BETTER THING would have been to take the antibiotics and ear drops and get into bed. Instead, I joined Cash at Molly's twenty-first birthday party. She answered the door in an apron, pointing to two pans of brownies: pot on the left, no pot on the right. A few minutes later, she stood on a chair to remove her apron and to issue an apology—it was no pot on the *left*, pot on the right. Everyone laughed. I couldn't remember which one I'd eaten from anyway. I felt as if there were pieces of broken glass in my ear, but I didn't want to miss out, so I sipped a beer on the couch and watched people dance.

Molly had a French bulldog, Cornelia—this was one of the reasons she lived off campus—and everyone else was so in love with Cornelia that I also put on a show about wanting to feed her treats from a jar. After a while, Cornelia settled by my feet, and I understood it, how good it felt to have that warm and loyal weight. I rubbed her ears and let her lick potato chip salt from my fingers. When I scanned the room to see if Molly was watching me, I saw that she was, once again, standing on a chair, but this time her hands were on Cash's shoulders, and she was talking while he nodded, his face serious.

I already had an excuse—my ear burned, and the cotton ball I'd stuffed into it was increasingly wet. I gave Cornelia a parting rub and stood up. I stepped over someone who muttered that I was interrupting his nap, and waved away the brownie someone else held up to my mouth. By the time I was on the front steps I could hear Cash following me. I moved faster, to give the impression that I wasn't waiting for him. He had taken a beer, and he swigged from it with exaggerated pleasure as we walked down the middle of the road.

"You could get a ticket for that open container," I said.

"From who? You?" Cash slowed to a stop, gesturing at the houses around us, duplexes with shallow front porches and two front doors, not unlike the place my father had lived in since the divorce. Molly's house was the only one full of noise and light; her neighbors probably wanted to sleep. The street itself was empty, and I kicked a pebble in front of me. He walked me all the way back to my dorm and watched me unlock the main door.

"What's going on with you and Molly?" I said.

"Nothing," he said. "How's the ear?"

"It hurts."

He hadn't bothered to zip his vest, and it hung open.

"Don't you ever get cold?" I said.

"Nope."

I held the heavy door open. He was still standing there.

"Are you coming up?"

"Just for a minute," he said.

How THIS WAS different from the countless other times he'd been in my room, I couldn't say. The way he closed the door and took his shoes off had a kind of finality to it. I turned on my lamp, then debated what would happen if I brushed my teeth. I feared that he would leave if I left the room, so I squeezed toothpaste directly into my mouth. It seemed that the only logical thing I could do was offer the tube to him, which I did. He rolled the paste around in his mouth, scowling.

"Is this *fennel*?" he said.

"Yes."

He tightened the cap and set it down on my desk. "You are the only person I know who would buy fennel toothpaste," he said.

I was afraid of frightening him. I sat on my bed with my hands behind my back. When he said, "Are you going to move over?" I pulled my shirt off and slid far under the sheet. He lay parallel to me, looking at my bare shoulder.

"You sleep with a skirt on?"

"No," I said. "Do you?"

"Ha." He got out of bed and undressed without looking at me.

Having built up the idea of sex with Cash for years, I found that I was scrambling too hard to remember it as it happened. I had too many questions—Did he kiss every girl's eyelids, or just mine? He moved so quickly that I struggled to keep up. It crossed my mind that he just wanted to get through it, to reach the other side. He had a condom, which meant that he always had condoms, which meant that I just happened to be the person with him. At one point the cotton ball fell from my ear and he put it back in.

He asked if he was hurting me, a reasonable question that struck me as an immense kindness, and I felt my eyes welling, and I shook my head no. I kept thinking of something I'd overheard at a party our sophomore year, a drunk guy talking to Cash about me. *Zuzu's vibe*, the guy had said, *is missionary with her eyes closed*. Cash said, *Wouldn't know*. I'd pretended not to hear.

I feared that the guy had been right, or that I was disappointing Cash somehow. Then I worried that the fear itself would be disappointing, and I made some theatrical sounds to convey how happy I was. The fact that I was happy seemed almost irrelevant.

I wanted to hear my name come out of his mouth; instead, I got one deep sigh from him, then he let his body drop onto mine. I rubbed his back. His head was on my chest, and I was an efficient and quiet crier, but he must have known. He asked if I was okay, and I said yes. He asked again if he had hurt me, and I said, emphatically, no.

I WOKE AT the sound of him pulling his shirt over his head around four in the morning. He was careful with the door, trying not to disturb me. In the hallway, I heard him exhale. He was leaving for London in two weeks.

His presence, I discovered as the sky began to grow light, had kept me from noticing the ruptured eardrum. The pain was hot and sharp, and I took two painkillers without water, even though their bitterness stayed on my tongue.

Lookout

December 10, 2002

Hours after Cash left my bed, I left it too. I got into my car without showering, wearing the Vineyard sweatshirt and a pair of bootcut corduroys that were too long. They dragged in the slush as I crossed the silent parking lot.

It was so early that the traffic lights were set to blinking red. BBC was on the radio. Stopping briefly at the open college gates, I wondered if I could talk to Molly, if we could set aside that it was Cash, our Cash, I was talking about. It wasn't a story of triumph. On the contrary, it was the story of how I couldn't stop thinking, how I'd ruined it even as it was happening.

I was desperate to talk to a woman, but that woman could not be Molly. Molly and Cash, as I saw it, were always about to get together. I sometimes felt that I was the one keeping them apart. I sometimes felt that I was, ultimately, irrelevant.

I HEADED HOME, a familiar route, the Taconic to the Mass Pike. My take-out cup of coffee flooded its lid every time I hit a pothole. I was planning to surprise Julia. She was taking business administration courses at the local community college and working part-time as an office manager for a graphic design firm. She had already moved in with Perry, a man she had met at a bar, which was the same way our parents had met. Both Trish and I, at different times, had made note of this in less-than-encouraging tones. I did so over the phone. "Not every woman in this family is waiting to be scooped up by a rich white man," Julia told me.

"I am *not*."

"What makes you think I'm talking about you?" she said.

Perry was taciturn and athletic, obsessed with his health—he steamed his vegetables—and clear about his professional goals. He was five years older than Julia. He commuted to Connecticut for his job as an engineer, and sometimes he slept at a coworker's apartment for a break from the Hartford rush hour.

The closer I got to Julia's exit, the more I dreaded the thought of Perry. Whatever people found charming in me, he didn't see it. I dreaded, too, how young and childish I sometimes felt in their apartment. The sight of her little shoes next to his enormous ones. The bed they shared, the two mugs in the sink. She had stumbled into real adulthood, and I lived in a dorm.

Taking the Ashworth exit off I-91, I began to feel embarrassed for not having bothered to shower. I flipped my visor mirror open and looked at myself, wild-haired, a panicked fugitive, and why? Because I'd gotten what I wanted. It made no sense. Julia would have to say, over and over, "I don't understand." I would have to admit that I didn't either.

JULIA'S DRIVEWAY WAS empty, but there was a ladder I recognized as my father's, leaning against one side of the house. I parked and left my motor running and my door open. My car was a gift from Glenn, and it was far too nice for someone whose only employment experience by that time was "writing tutor." I touched the ladder's rungs with my fingers, wincing at the cold.

The year of my parents' divorce, months before they told us, Dennis had repainted my bedroom ceiling. I had jokingly suggested that we throw glitter into the white paint, and he had gone out to the garage and returned with a jar of what looked like shredded gold. Why he owned it at all is something I've never understood. "Go ahead, throw it," he said. And while I made a mess, he steadied that ladder.

I LEFT JULIA'S and kept driving, crossing into a state park several miles away. There was a metal lookout tower there that my father had sometimes brought us to. I hadn't thought of it in years, but it suddenly felt that I'd driven two hours just to see it. In my clearest memory of the tower, Trish had refused to get out of the car because it was too cold, and Julia had agreed with her, but I followed my father up the steps, counting each one, until we reached the top. We could see our breath, and we could see the Connecticut River, deep and mellow, unmoved by us.

As I pulled up to the tower, I saw somebody was there already, in a hooded sweatshirt, smoking a cigarette. I was reluctant to be alone with him, or to negotiate the awkward business of passing him on the stairs. His truck stood in the only real parking space. I started backing up to make a tight three-point turn, but then he was coming down the stairs, waving his arms, frightening me.

"Zuzu!" he was saying.

It was Noel. I cracked the window.

"What are you doing here?" he said.

"Killing time. What about you?"

"You could say the same." He took his menthols from his pocket and offered me one. I suppose I was relieved—he was not a stranger who was going to hurt me—and there was a second type of relief, as I shifted into park and turned the car off and got out. It was a relief to be distracted from the matter of Cash.

It was windy and cold, but the hood of my car was warm, and we sat on it.

"I'm taking some classes at the CC," he said.

"Are you? That's good."

"Computer science." He made a face. "Boring but practical."

"Ha. I'm majoring in English, so. Boring and impractical."

He nodded. His cheeks were turning pink.

"Do you miss school?"

"Your current school, my former one? Yeah. Sure." He looked up at the sky and seemed to deliberate before he said, "Good parties. Too many good parties, in my case. Kind of forgot to do anything else."

I leaned back against the windshield. So far the season's snow had melted, leaving a few patchy islands, speckled gray. "Would you ever go back?"

"Me? Nah." He shook his head. "Not the right fit, as they say. I am still in touch with a bunch of people. Not you, Miss Zuzu, but some other people."

His leg was getting closer to mine. I slid off the hood and stood in front of him, stamping my feet.

"I have to get going," I said. "I still have papers due."

"We're not in high school, you know," Noel said, his eyes closed.

"Perfectly aware of that, thanks."

"I just don't want you thinking that things are the same." He opened his eyes then. "I'm dating someone."

"That's cool."

"Julia still likes to tease me, though, when I run into her."

"She thinks she's hilarious."

"I'm not like that anymore." He finally looked at me. "I'm not hung up on you."

I laughed. "Don't worry, Noel. I never thought you were hung up on me."

"Yeah, you did. Everybody did."

"You had a crush. It's not a big deal."

"It wasn't a crush."

"No?"

He shook his head.

"It was something else."

"Mysterious," I said. He looked at me steadily. He looked at me even as he was taking his truck keys from his back pocket.

"It really was something else," he said.

I DROVE THE two hours back to campus, in time to get a cup of to-mato soup at the dining hall. Half the school had already left for winter break; it was quiet and subdued, and there were laptops on every table. When I stopped in the student mail room I ran into Molly, who told me that Cash had left for home that morning. I told her I knew. Well, he was looking for you, she said. He was looking all over for you.

The Runner

September 4, 2003

He returned from England with longer hair, with a blur of a tattoo on his back whose meaning he refused to explain. He insisted on driving ten extra miles to the store that sold imported cans of beans in sauce, which he layered over wheat toast. He had been to every European city I could name. He had always been a tea drinker, but now he drank a different brand.

His months abroad had made the night we spent together feel far more distant than it was. My habit of sleeping with Ethan, a chemistry major and compulsive swimmer, had also made it seem more distant than it was. I muffled the thought of it by pressing my ear against Ethan's chest.

I OFTEN SAT on the bleachers while Ethan swam laps. A few weeks after classes started, Cash, who had taken up swimming, waved to me from the pool. He climbed out and walked over, goggles pushed into his hair, red high on his cheeks. He stood with his hands on his hips, which made him look young and uncertain.

"What are you doing here?" he said.

"Waiting for Ethan."

Cash shook his head so that droplets fell on me. "I'll be dressed in five minutes if you want to grab lunch or something."

"I can't." I pointed at the far lane. "I'm waiting for Ethan."

I watched the rigidity of his shoulders as he walked toward the men's showers. Did he hate to hear me say that? It seemed that he did.

Believing, as I did at the time, in infinitude, I thought I could draw it out. I thought I could feel that silent pull from Cash and still take what Ethan was offering me, which was a frank, unsentimental desire to have me in his bed. The first time he saw me naked, he reached for the clothes I'd thrown on his desk to find the size tag on my bra, then nodded to himself, as if he'd confirmed something important. It didn't feel as uncouth as it sounds. He was intensely curious about my body, and had limited, mostly feigned interest in what I had to say. This was a mutual condition. My project was only to feel desired.

Cash's return gave Ethan a second job, which was to torment Cash, simply by existing. When I didn't pick up my phone for several days in a row, I received an email from Cash: *Did you move in with that guy?* The only time Ethan happened to take my hand in his, we were walking from the pool back to his apartment, and Cash was walking toward us on the path. I saw him stop, turn, and duck into the art museum, a building he had visited only once, as far as I knew.

It pained me to do some of the things I did—to move my leg away from his underneath a table, even though we had often casually allowed ourselves to touch that way. To know that he was celebrating his twenty-second birthday at a bar, and to go, instead, to the city to stay at the Pierre with Ethan, whose parents couldn't use their reservation. At the hotel we drank too much champagne and fell asleep watching TV, and in the morning my headache was so bad that I didn't want him to touch me, and we slumped against each other holding coffees on the long Metro North ride back to school. I had nothing to say to him, so I rested my head on his shoulder and closed my eyes.

ONCE I WAS home, I called Cash to say that I was sorry I'd missed his party.

"You're in luck," he said. "Guess who's here?"

There was the fumbling sound of the phone being handed off to someone else.

"It's time we meet, my spy," Bronwen Cashel said.

"Oh, I'm a mess," I said. "I'm in my pajamas."

"Change into your running clothes and join me, would you? My lazy son won't come with me."

"Not lazy," Cash shouted in the background. "Hungover."

"What do you say, Zuzu? The library steps in ten?"

My "running clothes" were a pair of cotton shorts, a cotton T-shirt, and my tightest bra, but I ignored the pulse of my headache and put them on. I hadn't met Bronwen yet. I wanted her to like me as much as she seemed to think she did.

HER FRENCH BRAID contained the reds and golds of my sophomore year tapestry. She could not have weighed more than a hundred pounds, including the diamond studs in her ears and the socks on her feet. She was stretching when I approached her; her face was upside down, framed by the curve of her freckled arm, when she said my name. Cash had mentioned, once or twice, that she was from Virginia, and I thought I could hear Virginia in her voice.

"How'd you know it's me?" I said.

She straightened up.

"He has pictures of all of you at home," she said.

"All of you" meant all of his friends—I understood this—but I also understood that, in looking through her son's photographs, she had been looking for me in particular.

"Let's go," she said. I followed her. She walked briskly to the open gates, then asked if we should go left or right.

"Left," I said, because I wanted to sound decisive. She took off. I ran behind her, my breasts jostling uncomfortably. Waiting at the crosswalk of a two-way street felt like a great mercy. I stopped, wishing for water, while she jogged in place.

It was soon clear that I could not keep up with her. Her legs were heavily freckled, and she had the kind of spine you could see right through her shirt. She talked easily while I gasped for breath. She had, in addition to an expectation that she would be obeyed, a kind of intrinsic courtesy, and she slowed down for me. Half a mile away, residential streets already starting to turn to farmland, I considered drinking from the spigot on the side of a stranger's house because I was so thirsty. By three quarters of a mile, I had a cramp in my side and was slowing to a walk.

"Try breathing in through your nose, out through your mouth," she said. "We'll turn around at the next stop sign."

There was a small berry farm to our left and nothing but trees on our right. The road stretched before us, no stop signs in sight. I felt sweat in my eyes and on my upper lip. My jaw was tense. When I glanced at her she looked unbothered.

"All right," she said, slowing abruptly. "I guess there's no stop sign out here."

"Thank God," I said, without meaning to.

We turned in the direction we'd come from, and I spent a few minutes focused on the way each breath I took resulted in a bolt of warm pain. My limbs itched and they were sore. I'd have paid good money for ice water. Just under the discomfort was pleasure, and soon enough I started to relax. A liquid ease arrived in my limbs, and a burst of confidence, so that when Bronwen looked at me I said, "Why didn't you ask Molly? Molly likes to run."

"Which's one Molly again?" she said.

We walked in silence for a bit. I felt angry with my parents for raising me to spend my leisure time wandering shopping malls and eating sweets. There was an entire culture that I felt I'd arrived at too late to understand. Camping and hiking, tennis and skiing: We'd done none of that. We'd never had so much as a picnic in the grass of our own backyard. I'd lived in a house where the TV was usually on. Even when the house got bigger and nicer, the TV was on. The only thing that could draw us all outdoors was the beach.

"Zuzu," Bronwen said, once we were within view of the library. Cash was sitting on the steps, listening to his Discman, not looking at either of us. "My son isn't an especially talkative fellow."

"I've noticed."

"It's not my place to say anything."

I waited. The soreness was gone from my body.

"You two are so young you might think this happens a lot more often than it does." She looked up at me, holding a hand across her brow to block the sun. "Don't waste it, sweetheart," she said.

FOR ALMOST TWO hours, I walked around emitting a glow that I recognize, now, as the sight of a person who thinks they are loved. If I'd been wearing a skirt, or that cashmere swing coat, I would have twirled across the quad, imagining myself, from above, as a well-watered flower. I said good morning to every person I passed, including a pair of bewildered freshmen on skateboards. I did not think of Ethan at all.

I wondered when I would next hear from Cash, and what he

might say to me. When he knocked on my door that afternoon, I saw that he had Molly's dog, Cornelia, with him.

"Um," I said, opening the door, "this is definitely supposed to be an animal-free environment."

"It's just Cornelia." He unclipped her from her leash. She trotted across the swept floor, then settled in front of the bed.

"I spent the afternoon cleaning."

"She ain't dirty."

I frowned at him. I didn't like when he said "ain't," perhaps because it was so unlike him, perhaps because I couldn't predict when he'd do it. He ran his hand over the desk, then sat in my chair.

"It really is clean in here."

"I told you. So is Bronwen still around?"

"Nope. She hit the road after lunch." He pulled a treat from his pocket and offered it to the dog, who hurried over to him.

"What'd she say about our run?"

"She said it was good." His expression didn't change; there had been no *Don't waste it, sweetheart* for him. I flirted with indignation— Was she the kind of mother who expected another woman to take care of her son?—but I couldn't sustain my distaste. I liked the idea more than I disliked it.

"We had a nice long chat about you," I said.

"I'll bet." He tossed the leash in the air and caught it. "Want to take the dog for a walk with me?"

"Why can't Molly walk her own dog?"

"You know me. I'm good to my friends."

"Yeah, you're famous for that."

"Come on."

"Okay." I stood up. "Let's take the same route I took with your mom this morning."

"The boss says we're taking the same route she took this morning," he told Cornelia.

As we walked the path that led off campus, I offered to hold the leash.

"But you don't like dogs," Cash said.

"I do too." I wrapped the dirty red leash once around my wrist. Cornelia's strength surprised me, and I stumbled a bit. "You want to see where I ran with your mom?"

"Sure."

At the crosswalk, I waved my free hand in the air.

"I was already out of breath at this point," I said.

"Ha."

"I'm serious."

"It just takes practice," he said.

"Thanks, Coach."

"Did she run backward?"

"Did she what? No."

"Like this."

"You're going to get hit by a car."

"Not unless you let me get hit by a car."

Cornelia barked at him anxiously, then continued to explore the grass at the side of the road. I felt sweat on the back of my neck.

There was no way to have a conversation while he jogged backward, and because it was my job to keep him from being struck down, I barely looked at his face. We made it about five blocks before he took the leash from me—"Poor gal needs some *real* exercise," he said— and then he and the dog ran ahead. He stopped once, whistling and telling me to "hustle," but I wasn't going to run after him, not more than I felt I already had.

Denny

It was a typical death story—man in his sixties has heart attack while shoveling—and one of my first thoughts was that it would have amused my father, who always felt like an outsider, to have joined this brotherhood of Americans felled by yard work. A neighbor had seen him and sought help, but it was too late.

Julia was waiting for me to say something.

"Does Mom know?" I said.

"I'm calling her next."

"You're the designated caller, are you?"

"The hospital called me, Susan, because I was listed as next of kin."

I whistled.

"Next of kin. Good for you, Julia."

"You should sound sad." She sniffled. "Your father just died."

"I am exceedingly sad."

"I fell over," she said. "Perry had to sit on the floor with me. Oh, and don't worry about Betty. Daddy's neighbor wanted to take her."

"Who's Betty?"

"His *cat*."

"Right. I know. I just forgot."

She told me a few things I already knew: that our father had high cholesterol, and that it didn't stop him from a daily bag of potato chips with a full-sugar soda. That he thought drinking water was essentially pointless because it had no flavor. I was distracted by the image of Perry holding her on the floor, how quickly he must have knelt to comfort her.

"Perry used to make Daddy walk around the block after dinner," Julia said. "I think in the past few years he really never took a step unless he had to."

"I wouldn't know."

"Well. You would've had to call or visit in order to know what was going on with him."

"Maybe he didn't respond to phone calls from both of his daughters with, shall we say, equal levels of enthusiasm."

"Maybe calling once a year was insufficient."

"Maybe—"

"Stop," she said. "We shouldn't fight. Our father just died."

"Did he write us any letters or anything?"

"This was an *accident*, Zuzu. He didn't—"

"No, I know. I just heard that sometimes people write letters well in advance. Just in case."

"I have never heard of that in my life." She sighed. "Anyway. We have to figure out what kind of service we want—what kind of service *he* would have wanted. You'll probably have to come out here."

"Yeah," I said. "I'll come out there."

We always spoke as if to get from the Hudson Valley to western Massachusetts was to undertake an arduous journey, to encounter some kind of challenging terrain, when in truth it took only two hours by car, a bit longer when the highways were clogged with people out to see the autumn leaves.

When Agnes got out of the shower, I was standing at our bedroom window.

She pulled the halves of her wet ponytail to tighten it.

I told her about my father, but I must have spoken too quietly, because she said that she was afraid she'd misheard me. I said it again.

"Oh, Zuzu," she said. "Oh, no."

She sat on the end of our bed and I stayed at the window, watching the husband in the house across the street bring the trash bins out to the curb. This duty had fallen to me, almost without exception, from our first week in the house. Agnes had done it twice in the years we'd lived on Carmel Lane: once when I had a migraine, and once when Gideon had an ear infection and I'd gone to bed early, because I was sleeping on his floor.

I wanted not to think about the trash, not then. I pulled back from the window and looked at my wife. A wet spot had formed on her silk robe, between her shoulder blades.

"What can I do?" she said.

I shook my head.

"I'm here if you need me."

She was saying the right things—I had no rational complaint—but I felt, however unfairly, that she was failing me. She went downstairs to make herself an omelet for dinner, and I went into our closet to get a photo of my father. The silver paint was flaking off the frame. It had been taken in 1988, when my father still had plentiful hair. The four of us had gone to a portrait studio in Springfield, where we were ignored, in spite of our two o'clock appointment, until my mother figured out that the manager sometimes went fishing with her brother, after which the photographer was stiffly polite, at least to her. When I pulled the photo free of the frame I saw that she'd written *Denny & T* on the back.

Denny & T sounded younger and more joyful than these people. Denny had a handlebar mustache, and a wool vest over his shirt, with orange and brown chevrons at the V. Five days after the picture was taken, he would get hired to manage a new branch of a national discount store, the job he would keep for the rest of his life. T's eyelids were shadowed purple, her cheeks rounder than she would have liked, and the gold crucifix she wore over her pink sweater was not so much a testament to her faith as it was proof that sometimes her parents tried to buy her nice things.

I looked at them and pitied them: for being ignored when they arrived, and for wearing cheap clothes, and for having daughters who fought the entire ride home, and for my mother, who burned the dinner (sticky chicken, lima beans, canned biscuits) because she was arguing with Denny about tipping the photographer. I pitied them for choosing, as their portrait background, a covered bridge over misty water with a horse-drawn carriage in the distance.

I stared at the photograph, then took a picture of it and sent it to Cash, who sent back a series of question marks.

My parents, I wrote.

I could tell he was drafting responses. Finally he wrote, Didn't recognize your mom.

It's the hair, I wrote. God bless the 80s.

Indeed. Did you send this just for fun?

I wanted to write *yes*. Writing *yes* kept things as they had been with my father—tense and unresolved, but not without possibility.

Actually, I wrote. Actually not.

Cash waited.

Actually, I typed, after misspelling the word several times, I just found out that my father died.

I wanted him to call, and I did not want him to call. I had cried in front of him only once in my life.

I waited for, and received, a canned response two minutes later: Molly and I send our condolences to you and your family.

Thank you, I wrote. I took a screenshot and sent it to Julia, who wrote back immediately:

Why did you send me this?

I thought you'd want me to share condolences.

I don't even know who Molly is, she wrote.

Dennis Braeburn Visits the Vegetarian House

January 26, 2002

My father visited once, my sophomore year. I decided to host a dinner party in his honor, mostly to show him that I ate things like quinoa and hummus, and that I had managed to collect a handful of good-looking friends. I bought a mop so the kitchen floor would shine. Molly brought me flowers in an empty milk jug and Cash came to the table with comb tracks in his wet hair. He called my father "sir." Everyone shook my father's hand.

"Quite a formal gang we have here," he said, as if manners surprised him. He was the one who had taught me how to shake a hand.

I placed, just north of his plate, the recent copy of the student paper that featured something I'd written: a profile of a visiting writer. I'd used words I was proud of knowing—dichotomy, peripatetic.

"Well, someone likes to see her name in print, doesn't she?" he said, moving the paper out of the way to make room for his glass. Cash looked at me the way he sometimes did, to confirm I was okay.

My father winked at me—to take the sting out, I thought—but it didn't work. I looked at the candles I had lit for him in all my eager, stupid hope. The conversation shifted to television, and my father told the only story about me he shared that evening: how I had campaigned ceaselessly for cable, how I had claimed to "need" MTV, starting in second grade. Molly made an impassioned declaration of love for PBS, even when it was boring, and this led to my father's exhausting description of a nature series he'd watched.

Dessert was out-of-season strawberries and a box of canelés. My father made his only joke of the evening—"I'm sure none of you have ever tasted rum before"—and everyone laughed too hard, too long, to push us closer to the evening we'd wanted, the evening I'd wanted.

AFTER DINNER, I walked my father over to the campus art museum. I should have known better; it was late, and he had a two-hour drive ahead of him. He held the glass doors open for me with quiet forbearance, and I realized that I had mapped one of Molly Pierce's stories onto my poor father's body. Molly Pierce's father had brought pink champagne, even though she was nineteen, and macarons, because she loved them, and they had a picnic on the quad, just the two of them, and then they walked arm in arm through the museum galleries, and they had a code word for "overrated," which they whispered frequently, and which caused them both to laugh.

I hurried us through the rooms. I couldn't remember what I'd thought would impress him.

"You don't have to run," my father said.

I did have to run. We were back outside in fifteen minutes, standing by his car, which had one of those anti-theft locking bars on its steering wheel. He asked me where to stop for a coffee on the way back to the Taconic. I named a gas station and watched him buckle his seat belt and adjust his eyeglasses before he rolled the window down.

"Congratulations, Susan," he said.

Surprise

December 5, 2009

By my 1L winter, Cash and I spoke less and less often, and our text exchanges often felt perfunctory and dull; how are you, fine, how are you, fine. He had changed jobs, moved to a private equity firm. I didn't really know that meant, or what he did.

During the week between end of classes and start of exams, Cash called and asked me to attend his cousin's engagement party. Agnes had a strict library schedule—eight to eight—but I studied on our futon, where I had access to cooking shows. Watching someone else grate ginger and juice limes made me feel that I, too, could complete the task I'd set before myself.

"You can't find a real date?" I said.

"Ha," he said. "It's going to be at a restaurant like three stops away from you."

"So this is all about convenience?"

"Just come," he said. "I won't know anyone there."

"I thought it was your cousin."

"Second cousin on my mom's side. All people from Virginia, and I've met them like once."

"I have to study."

"Quit stalling," Cash said. "You know you're going to come."

I WAS NOMINALLY offended by movies and TV shows in which women obsessed over clothing—even if I loved to watch them, I claimed to know better than to follow their example—but after the call ended it seemed to me that I no longer had exams. I had one goal, and it was to find a dress that would startle Cash somehow, that would make him say something I could carry around.

There is no dress like that. A dress does nothing. It didn't stop me from forgoing two days of studying, wandering in and out of every kind of store: high-end boutiques; luxury consignment; cheap, flashy places that I could have found in a mall back home.

ON SUNDAY NIGHT, when Agnes came home from the library, I was standing in front of our closet.

"My mom always said legs or cleavage but never both," I told her.

She set her books down and sighed.

"Excuse me?"

"I need a dress. For the thing with Cash."

"Oh. You can borrow whatever you want," she said.

It hadn't occurred to me to borrow something from Agnes, whose wardrobe was not as tweedy and conservative as I'd thought when we met. She favored florals, long skirts, eyelet trim. I found most of it young, romantic, and overly girlish, but I didn't want to insult her, so I said I'd look. In the closet we shared, lit by the improbable chandelier, I found one I'd never seen her wear. It was gray silk, plain at the front, with a lace panel set in the back. It would have looked beautiful on Agnes, whose muscular shoulders I had been noticing more than I was precisely comfortable with. I had been late to a waxing appointment earlier that week because I stalled, knowing that Agnes was due home from hot yoga, knowing that her entire upper body would be flushed and wet and that she would peel her bra off in the hallway and drop it on the floor and it would lie there, forgotten, until I teased her about it.

I held the gray silk up to my chest.

"This is gorgeous," I said. "Where'd you get it?"

"Funny. My mom bought me that one. Doesn't appeal to me at all."

"Do you mind if I—"

"It's yours," she said.

THE LACE HAD been faintly irritating while I was getting ready—mascara, clear lip gloss, Chanel Allure—and as I walked to the subway the friction of the panel against my skin felt worse and worse. I tried to stand perfectly still on the train, but it didn't help, and once I was back in the fresh air, I shrugged the coat off to feel the cold.

Approaching the restaurant, I stopped to read a new text from Agnes.

> AGNES: okay now I'm taking a study break
> AGNES: wish you were around
> AGNES: woe is me
> AGNES: I am making cupcakes, what kind do you want

I was standing in front of a bodega. I went inside, found the aisle with cake mixes and canned frostings, and bought an assortment of sprinkles and sparkling sugars to bring home after Cash's cousin's party. I took a right out of the bodega instead of a left, which meant I was heading back to the subway, which I hadn't exactly intended to do, but I kept going, through the turnstile and right onto the waiting train, reasoning that I could drop everything off with Agnes, and then I could go back and engage in painful small talk with Cash's family: I was just there as a friend, we had met in college, and no I wasn't his date, and no we weren't dating, and I couldn't keep up with his mother on a leisurely run, and the dress I was wearing wasn't even mine.

AGNES WAS PLACING muffin liners into the tin when I came in. Muffin tins were the type of impractical, storage-gobbling items her parents sent—not new from the store, but exhumed from a deep closet somewhere in Marin County. She made fun of the package when it arrived, but she'd made cupcakes several times since she'd received it.

"Hey," she said when I let myself in. "What happened?"

"I got you these." I put the bag of sprinkles and sugar on the table.

"You're not going to the party?"

I scratched at my back.

"I guess the lace is bothering me," I said.

I fumbled with the hook and eye at the nape of my neck, and she came around and unzipped the dress, then held my upper arm so that I could step out of it. Fearing it would be visible through the lace panel, I hadn't worn a bra. She pressed her hand to the place where the lace had been, and she kissed the place where the lace had been, and I turned and I kissed her.

Where Have You Been

December 6, 2009

CASH: well well well

CASH: someone was too busy to show up last night

ZUZU: I'm SO sorry, was hanging out with Agnes,

lost track of time

CASH: haha no big deal

CASH: meet me at café in 30? I'll send the address

I HAD WOKEN up next to Agnes Blair for the first time. I knew there was nothing wrong about getting up, getting dressed, and having a coffee with Cash—in fact I felt I owed it to him, since I'd skipped the party completely—but I saw myself in the mirror as I buckled my belt. I looked like a guilty woman, sneaking out of the wrong house.

THE CAFÉ WAS unremarkable, and he was not even inside it. He was standing outside the café, yawning behind his hand.

"Miss Zuzu." He gave me a high five. "Finally, she arrives when she says she will."

"I said I was sorry."

"I'm just messing with you. Anyway." He stretched his arms over his head. "I've been subletting the last few weeks, working out of the New York office, but I have to pack up and head back to Boston tonight, and I figured we could hang out while I do that."

"You've been living here?"

"Just for a few weeks."

"How many?"

"I don't know." He looked up at the sky. "I guess twelve."

"Three months? You hid from me for three months?"

"There was no hiding involved."

"Why didn't you tell me? What have you been doing?"

"Working. Going to the gym. Happy hour. Three-for-ten tacos."

"I'm serious, Cash."

"So am I."

"We've been living in the same city." I waved my arms in the air. *Deranged albatross*, I thought. "The same city, and you didn't tell me."

"The fact that my job sometimes brings me to New York is not a personal affront to you."

"I wish it had seemed worth it to tell me you were here."

"I have a job. You're a law student. We are both busy people."

"Not too busy for the gym. Not too busy for three-for-ten tacos."

"You're right," he said. "I should have *no* life outside of work and

Zuzu. I should have reported to you immediately as soon as I left the office each day."

I thought of Agnes, who had still been sleeping when I left. I'd written a note saying that I was going out for coffee, which was turning out to be truer than it had been when I wrote it.

"I need to buy coffee," I said, motioning for him to move.

"Now you don't want to help me pack?"

"I never wanted to help you pack."

I went into the café to get in line, and he stood beside me for a while with his hands in his pockets. I ordered two Americanos and he ordered an egg on a roll and a grapefruit juice, which he drank while he was waiting for his change. I wanted to tell him about Agnes then. I wanted him to be curious about my mouth, which felt swollen, or the way I had raked my hair to one side without washing it, in a way that suggested, at least to me, that I had not spent my night alone.

"I guess I should go if you're delivering coffees to people," he said, glancing at the cups in my hands. "Oh, shoot. My mom asked me to get her one and I forgot."

"Bronwen's here?"

"Helping me pack."

"How much help do you need?"

"More than most people." He said this with a kind of pride.

"Here," I said. "She can have mine."

"You bring it while I wait for my sandwich." He touched the rim of the cup. "You know Bronwen loves her spy."

"Where do you even *live*?"

"Oh, God, don't get mad." He pointed at the ceiling. "Fourth floor."

THE DOOR TO Cash's sublet was propped open with boxes. Bronwen was sitting on the rug, zipping a duffel bag, and she didn't look up when she spoke.

"You're late, Molly darling."

"No, sorry," I said. "It's me."

"Zuzu!" She reached for the Americano I offered her. "Oh, thank God." She closed her eyes and took a long sip. "How've you been? Everything going well?"

My infrequent exchanges with Bronwen had always been in the same register—a warmth that was almost flirtatious, as if the way Cash spoke to me informed his mother's voice. I had, on occasion, wanted to know how it felt to receive maternal attention from Bronwen Cashel. Her body had made his body; this made it impossible for me to look at her without intense curiosity. I took note of her clothing, as I always did—khakis, boots, and a white-collared shirt with the sleeves rolled up. Her necklace lay under the shirt and could only be glimpsed when she turned a certain way: I could see the shape of a pendant, but not its stone.

"So you're waiting for Molly?" I said.

"Oh, I never know what's going on. You know James tells me

nothing. And you're in *law* school!" She looked relieved to have remembered. "How is law school?"

"Hard."

"I can just see you in the courtroom," she said, but she didn't know me well enough to "see" me anywhere. She turned her attention back to the duffel, unzipping it, nodding at its contents, zipping it again. "God forbid he can't find his sunscreen," she said. I resisted her; I didn't want to joke about how good it felt to indulge her son. I brought Agnes's coffee up to my cheek for the warmth of the cup.

"Is he on his way up, or?"

"I don't know," I said. "He doesn't actually tell me anything either."

She sat on the floor to stretch. I had a faint headache from the effort it took not to look around, to take in no details of the place he'd been living. Agnes was waiting for me—beautiful, clear, unrestrained Agnes, who didn't pretend, as far as I could tell, about anything. It felt wrong to stand there, wrong to let her coffee cool in my hand.

"I'm exhausted after last night—we had a little party," Bronwen said. "I'm so tired you can't trust anything I say." She laughed, but her posture of flightiness didn't suit her. You could, in fact, trust everything Bronwen said, and she'd said that Molly was late.

"I have to bring this to someone," I said, shaking Agnes's coffee so hard that it sloshed onto my wrist.

When Bronwen hugged me, I didn't lift my arms. I felt petulant and ridiculous, but I also felt that she, too, had been fooling me— her "spy" who knew nothing at all. She stood in the doorway to call out, "Good luck!" as I went down the stairs. I received it as a gentle push, to help me get just a bit farther away.

Out on the sidewalk, I feared running into Cash, but he wasn't there, and my fear took on its next shape. I decided it was better not to try to avoid her; it was better to let her walk by. She walked by without seeing me as I browsed a used bookstore's outdoor table. Under a loosely tied trench coat, Molly wore almost precisely the same outfit as Bronwen. She stood out from the other people on the street not because I knew her, but because she was smiling, she could not keep her good fortune off her face.

Forgiveness

January 3, 2010

A few weeks later, I received a postcard with a picture of the Tobin Bridge. Cash hadn't signed it, but I recognized his handwriting.

Dearest Z: Just making sure you know where I live.
P.S. CALM DOWN it's a joke. Come visit.

A few days later I bought one of the Williamsburg Bridge for him, but it made me feel disloyal to Agnes, with whom I was sleeping every night. I didn't know what to write. I carried the postcard around in my bag for a while. One afternoon, when we were at the New Museum, Agnes needed somewhere to spit her gum, and I gave her the postcard, and she neatly folded it over the gnawed-up wad of sugar-free strawberry. She threw it out somewhere on the Bowery.

Flower Problem

My father had been at the margins of my life for so long that I was able to forget about my loss for hours at a time. In the morning I made Gideon's oatmeal and used a cookie cutter to shape his apple and cheese sandwich into a star, a holdover from his preschool days that he still liked. I held up two small bags of chips—tortilla or potato?—and when he said both, I slipped them into his backpack next to the store-bought valentines he'd addressed to each of his classmates. When Agnes offered to drop him off at school, it took me a minute to realize that she was offering because she felt bad for me, because my father had died.

"I'll just leave the car at the station after," she said. "You know where the spare keys are?"

I did. I was never the one who lost the keys.

I waved to my wife and son from the front door in my bathrobe, the kind of tableau I had mostly witnessed through the windshield, because I was always the one who brought Gideon to school.

I emptied the dishwasher.

"Your dad died," I said, to hear it out loud.

My phone was in my back pocket, and I felt a text come through. It was from Cash: What kind of flowers am I supposed to get.

I sent him a series of question marks.

CASH: sorry that was for Molly. She wants me to
send you flowers

ZUZU: very sweet, but you don't need to send me flowers

CASH: yes I do

CASH: also I'm worried I ruined it by asking you what kind

ZUZU: I don't even really like flowers

ZUZU: you want to make me happy, send me some
condolence marzipan

Molly and Zuzu

~~

May 4, 2002

We were outliers in our group, Molly and I; neither of us had a best female friend. Living together did little to bring us closer. I was better at cleaning up, she was a better cook. She liked to play music at all hours. I bought earplugs. She was, she said, a "games" person, but I started to fidget at the thought of fixed rules. I liked to sit around and drink without a plan. Hungover, Molly insisted the best remedy was the gym. Sometimes I joined her, gagging as the elevation increased on my machine, but it was always worth it for the stack of buttered toast she made after, the eggs scrambled with chives and red pepper flakes.

There was, of course, the matter of Cash. Sometimes, when she ran into me as I left his room, she looked at me steadily, without questions, as if she had been able to see through the door while it was closed. She would often have seen us on his futon, lying there, talking or trying to study, or—it still pains me to recall this—he would read the paper and I would pretend to read the paper, just because I liked the way it felt to be next to him.

WHEN I RAN into Molly leaving Cash's room, I had no idea what I'd missed. I couldn't see through the door when it was closed.

IN THE SPRING, a few weeks before we all had to move out, Molly suggested we go to a bar alone, just the two of us. She stood in my doorway with her arms over her head, reaching for a pull-up bar that wasn't there. Cash had one; I didn't.

"We could do the frozen margarita place that he never wants to go to," she said.

"Margaritas are the worst," Cash called from down the hall.

She rolled her eyes and looked at me.

"Okay," I said.

On the walk over, I eyed her with suspicion. We were friends by implication, association, and proximity, but there was no natural warmth between us. I feared she would find me boring, even as I found her conversation meandering and vapid. She was smart, but she wasn't catty. When I tried to prod her into discussing people we knew in common, she kept saying they were "so funny" or "so great." *Where is the acid here?* I thought. She had no sharpness, no strangeness. She flickered with good health.

We got drunk enough for the ceiling to spin, drunk enough to cry.

Walking home with our arms linked, we traded confessions: You're beautiful, I told her. Oh, so are *you*, she said. I grabbed both of her hands. I love Cash so much, I told her. I know, she said. So do I.

In the morning, I felt ashamed at how I had exposed myself, and I expected Molly to share this concern. I still hold the image of her coming downstairs freshly showered, in a blue romper and mirrored aviators. She had cut herself shaving, and there was a spot of blood on her leg; when someone pointed it out to her, she licked her thumb and rubbed at it, then brought her thumb back to her mouth. My stomach had turned watching this. I hated her comfort with her body. In the residual spark and thirst of the previous night, some things seemed too clear to me: for instance, if you were choosing between the two of us, you would choose the one who thought she deserved you.

Good Imagination

~

One of Gideon's friends was throwing a Valentine's Day pizza party that evening, and Agnes surprised me by offering to pick him up on her way home. She'd taken an earlier train than usual, which she described, over text, as teeming with roses in cellophane. I let myself climb into bed at seven thirty to message back and forth with Julia, who wanted me to help her plan "a remembrance of Daddy." Agnes and I had agreed to proceed with our long weekend plans, especially since Gideon already had a place to be; we did not want him in a room full of weeping people. We'd still drive to eastern Mass to see Heidi, and at some point I'd see Cash in Boston, but we'd go to western Mass first, for my father's memorial. I felt queasy anxiety over how my father's service fit neatly into our plans, as if it were just a quick stop on a road trip. It would have felt more virtuous to shift things around for him—to cancel and rearrange, to agonize over how to do it. But we could do it easily.

WHEN THEY GOT home, Gideon came in first, to give me the cinnamon heart candies he'd promised to save for me.

"Love you, G," I said.

"Love you, Mommy." He looked down at the red stain the candy had made on his hands. "Are you sad about it?"

I wanted not to scare him. To say yes, I thought, might scare him. To say no might scare him more.

"I am sad, but I'm okay," I said. He nodded, looking relieved. Once he was back in the hallway, he began to skip, high on sugar and his Thursday-night party. When we'd told him about my father, he asked if it was okay that he didn't remember ever meeting him.

I WAS ALWAYS glad when Agnes wore dry-clean-only clothes to work because she was more likely to hang them up. She put the dress on a hanger, but she peeled off her stockings—a sure sign that she'd gone to court—and left them in a crumpled ball on the armchair, where they would stay until I moved them. She stood in her underwear and bra, a band of pink across her stomach from the elastic top. An argument felt imminent, if for no other reason than that she had already stated, four times, that she hadn't eaten all day. An argument felt inevitable once I told her that we had to go to Julia's early.

"For planning," I said.

"You want us to go tomorrow?"

"Yeah."

"I have work. Gideon has school."

"I know that, Agnes."

She squinted at her phone, shaking her head. "There are meetings I cannot miss. *Cannot* miss."

"So I'll go alone. I'll take Amtrak and you drive out Saturday, after you drop Gideon off at Theresa's."

She nodded and brought her phone almost to her nose.

"The Vermonter, the Vermonter," she said, looking for my train. I dozed while she bought my ticket. She said something several times, something that sounded like "black wool."

I opened my eyes. "Excuse me?"

"Black wool for the service?"

I sat up.

"I guess so? I don't really know what 'the service' is. It's Julia's show."

"That's sounding a *little* bitter," Agnes said.

I watched her pull my plain cotton underpants from the top drawer: a pair for the night at Julia's, and one for the night at Heidi's; another for the following night, which we were planning to spend at my mother's before heading home, mostly to break up the drive. Watching Agnes fold my flannel pajama pants, I understood that she was trying to be kind—it was objectively kind to pack a suitcase for your possibly grief-stricken wife. I watched her choose shirts that were too cropped and too tight for my comfort, but I didn't want to argue about it. I set my alarm for five thirty, knowing she would sleep through it, and that I could quietly switch out her choices in the morning before I left.

THE FIRST TIME she packed a suitcase for me, we were going to the christening of my cousin's baby. My family declined their invitations to the christening, largely because it required flying to Omaha in the middle of winter. I agreed to go if my mother and stepfather would pay for Agnes and me. For some reason I thought it would be a romantic trip.

In fact, it was not romantic. We were unprepared for the cold of the Great Plains. We were unprepared to feel so out of place even though so many people were kind. We shivered in the church, and I lost the nerve I thought I'd come with; instead of introducing Agnes as my wife to distant aunts and uncles, I said either "this is Agnes" or nothing at all. When we checked in at the hotel, the clerk seemed not to believe, at first, that the two of us shared a last name, even after we showed our IDs. At night, we called the front desk to ask if there was a way to make the heating unit surpass eighty degrees. It was impossible to get warm enough.

I ventured to the pool alone one morning—Agnes hadn't packed a suit, saying it would be too cold, even indoors—and I saw that an older woman was already swimming laps. She stopped, treading water in the deep end, to ask me if I knew whether or not the hotel required bathing caps. She herself was not wearing a bathing cap, and I understood her question perfectly, which was not a question at all. She didn't want my hair in her pool. I got in anyway, but I climbed out after a few short laps. She was mostly treading water and watching me.

When I returned to the room and told Agnes, she demanded that I get out of my wet suit and into a hot shower. I was glad to subject myself to her bossy caretaking, and I was standing under the hot spray, soaping my body, when I heard the heavy door click.

"Agnes?" I said, but she didn't answer. When I rinsed and stepped out in a towel, my bathing suit wasn't where I'd left it, hanging on the knob. I sat on the edge of the bed, letting my hair drip onto the blanket, and flipped through channels on the TV until she returned, my wife, wearing only my cold, wet bathing suit, with a long-sleeve shirt open over it.

"The bitch wasn't there anymore," she said.

"What bitch?"

"The one harassing you at the pool."

"Why did you change though? Were you going to swim after her?"

She looked down at herself, as if she only then realized what she wore, and we both started to laugh, and she jumped on top of me, knocking me flat on the bed, and my head filled with the scent of the chlorine that had been on my body and was now on her body.

"Why did I change," she gasped, tears from laughter starting to flow. "Why did I change?"

Our hotel room had a view of a bridge, and Iowa stood on its other side. Iowa: Our marriage counted there. If something bad happened to one of us, we said—if, for instance, one of us needed a hospital—the other would have to carry her over the bridge, so that the state would agree that we were each other's wives. New York did not agree, at that time, that we were each other's wives. It was an indignity we were used to, but it felt sharper when we were so close to ground we could stand on as married women. On occasion people called Agnes my partner, even when I said "wife," and it felt like a slight, or like they didn't quite believe me, or like they were offering a gentle correction.

The Snap

On Friday morning I bought a coffee in Penn Station, then saw a rat scuttle behind a row of bins and threw the cup away. Agnes had packed two granola bars and an apple in a brown lunch bag for me, which made me feel cared for, but which I now associated with the sight of the rat. On the way to board the Vermonter I wound up pitching the bag into a trash can; it was too easy for me to imagine unrolling its top to find a rodent inside.

On the train, I dozed until we emerged into the sunlight, at which point I woke from the snap of a mousetrap. I was both aware that this was impossible and certain that it had happened. It had happened around 1990, in the kitchen in Ashworth. We had a beaded curtain in the pantry doorway, and my father, having just baited a trap with peanut butter, hoisted me into the air at the sight of a tiny creature. Then we heard the snap, while the beads swung gently back and forth and the air smelled thickly of peanuts.

Don't worry. I'm sure it didn't hurt, he'd said. Even then, in his arms, I felt that he truly misunderstood me. Perhaps he had confused me with Julia, the daughter who might have worried about the mouse.

Don't worry. I'm sure it didn't hurt, to the daughter who would have set a trap in every room.

WE DIDN'T UNDERSTAND each other, I sometimes said about my father. Yes, he did fatherly things. He doled out allowance—two dollars a week into an empty marinara jar. He put together my first bicycle, with streamers and a basket.

He was impatient, and quick to let me know I had ruined things. He seemed particularly worried that I would ruin things for Julia. Even before my parents divorced, I could see that he found Julia easier to manage. Handing me a dish of ice cream, he used to say, *This is it, Susan,* but it never worked, I always wanted more.

A FEW MINUTES before my train arrived in Springfield, I received a text from my sister.

The window guy is here early. Perry is out running errands. Sending Noel to pick you up.

No, I wrote. I'll ask Mom.

Too late, baby, she wrote. He's on his way.

NOEL RAFFERTY WAS waiting for me next to my sister's car. He was underdressed, in a peach-colored flannel shirt and no jacket. His jeans were light blue, unfashionably light, held in place by a braided belt. His white sneakers, I determined at a glance, were new. His hairline had receded slightly. He had gone through a long-haired, bearded, hemp-necklace stage, but that had been almost ten years ago. He was none of the things I might have casually suggested in high school—not hideous, not a loser. He was a tall guy holding a set of keys. He should have been wearing a coat.

"You look displeased, Zuzu," he said. He stepped forward to take my suitcase by the handle. Our knuckles brushed.

"I could have just gotten an Uber."

"Her window guy showed up early."

"Yes, I heard all about the window guy."

He placed my suitcase in the trunk, then walked to the passenger-side door and held it open for me. I hadn't expected this, and it took me a minute to understand. I shook my head.

"It's my sister's car," I said. "I'm driving."

"Suit yourself." He tossed me the keys.

WHY HAD I insisted that I drive? I regretted it by the time he had buckled himself in beside me, settling against the window to watch me tilt the mirrors.

"You can adjust the steering wheel," he said.

"I know that." I didn't. I sat back to let him shift the wheel into a better position. I wondered if it thrilled him, to be so close to me.

Julia had a vanilla-and-cinnamon air freshener tied to her rear-view mirror. By the time I merged onto I-91, I was nauseated by the scent. I rolled down the windows.

"Not cold enough for you?" Noel said.

"Guess not."

"Oh. Also. I'm sorry about your dad."

"Thank you."

He scratched his jaw, then studied his lap.

"You look like you don't live here anymore."

"I don't. Thank God."

"You look like you never *did* live here though."

I shrugged.

"You've always looked that way, now that I think about it. Like you're from somewhere else. Somewhere fancier."

"Let's not talk about how I look."

"Okay. Fair." He leaned his head against the window and closed his eyes. I didn't like the intimacy this suggested; that he and I would drive around in a car while he dozed. I turned on the radio and listened to an ad for a furniture store.

"I heard you were still maybe going to be a lawyer," he said, lifting his head from the window.

"False," I said. "Where'd you hear that from?"

"Julia."

"She probably said I was thinking of taking the bar again, which . . . no. I'm not." I slapped the steering wheel. "That ship has sailed for me."

"Maybe for the best." He smiled. "Nobody likes lawyers."

"Well. I went to law school and I'm married to a lawyer, Noel."

"Okay. Apparently, you love lawyers."

"Yep."

"I forgot you were married to a . . . I'm sorry. Believe it or not, I don't think of you very often."

"I believe it," I said.

We crossed the Connecticut River and passed the cluster of old silk mills, their broken windows sparkling in the sun. Within five minutes, we'd driven by a cornfield and an orchard. I entered an empty rotary and went around the circle twice, passing the Ashworth City Hall, where I'd married Agnes.

PERRY AND JULIA's house was a 1980s saltbox-style modular home. It had gray vinyl siding, red shutters, and an enviable yard. They had chosen it over more charming homes because of the second-floor in-law suite with its separate entrance—what Perry called a "guaranteed income source." This was where Noel lived.

There were multiple trucks in the driveway when we arrived, including Noel's—they'd parked him in, he explained, which was why he'd borrowed Julia's car—and several people on ladders. Some of the windows had needed replacement for over a year.

"Shall we?" Noel said.

"How long do you think they're going to be here?" I said. "I sat on a train all morning. I really need a shower."

"Not long. Probably another half an hour. By the way. It's not my place to say, but . . . she's nervous."

"About?"

"The memorial. She's worried you won't like her ideas, or that you won't think it's enough."

"What do you two do, sit up and talk all night?"

"Sometimes, yeah."

I turned in the seat to give him my full, critical attention.

"I'm not Julia," I said. "I don't want to sit here and have a heart-to-heart with you."

"I wasn't trying to have a—"

"If my sister is worried about something, she can tell me herself."

"Fair," he said.

"*Fair. Fair. Fair. Fair.* You love that, don't you."

"Pretty sure I've said it only twice." He laughed, a dry squawk I remembered from high school. He got out of the car, opened the trunk, carried my suitcase over the paved walkway—to keep its wheels dry, I guessed. He returned to open the driver-side door for me.

"Tell you what," he said. "You want to take a shower, you can use mine upstairs."

"I—"

"What if I sit out here in the car until you're done?"

"I might take you up on that," I said.

I followed him through a side entrance, up a set of poorly lit stairs, and into his living room.

"So, I didn't think you'd be coming here," he said, rushing past me to gather clothes from his couch.

"You shouldn't clean for me."

"Just wait there."

I stayed where I was, noticing the place's various incongruities—wood paneling lit by the warm glow of wall-mounted sconces; a table with two folding chairs and, in its center, a ceramic bowl overflowing with grapes. The couch had several blankets on it, as if he habitually slept there, although I could see, through a partially opened door, that he had a bed. The bed had been made in a way I disliked, with the blankets and sheets drawn up over the pillows, creating a lump that could never be properly smoothed and evened. There was a vacuum on the floor next to the bed, as if it had fallen over.

"All right," he said. "Take your time."

"Yeah. I wasn't going to rush for you."

He tilted his head. "Were you always like this?"

"Like what?"

"Snappy? Abrasive?"

"I feel like I shouldn't use your shower now."

"It's fine to use my shower," Noel said. "But you could also try talking to me with, like, maybe *slightly* less contempt."

"I'm sorry, Noel," I said.

"Let's not worry about it."

"I don't need a shower. It's fine. I can wait."

"You're still welcome to use it."

I shook my head.

"I'm just out of sorts," I said. "Sad, you know, about my dad."

"Of course you are."

I waited for him to burrow deeper into his forgiveness. I wanted him to tell me that I could do whatever I wanted, and say whatever I wanted, because I was in mourning. Instead, he said he had errands to run.

Alone, I felt drained of the urge to go through his things. I thought of the time in college he'd referred to us as "mutts," how angry I'd been, and how that anger had mostly been my fear that someone would overhear him. It wasn't a kind word for a person; worse, it wasn't a pretty word. It did not mean pretty, it did not mean desirable.

I washed my face with cold water at Noel's kitchen sink. Unzipping my suitcase, I saw that I'd forgotten to switch out the clothes Agnes had packed for me. Everything my wife had chosen was a size too small, which meant she'd pulled from the left side of my closet, where I kept the items that were too nice to give away. The loosest thing was a cable-knit sweater dress with a coffee stain at the hem, and I pulled it on, tugging in search of a way to get comfortable.

Real Grieving

I let myself into Julia's house.

Our mother was in the kitchen, shredding leftover rotisserie chicken. Julia was at the table, staring at her laptop. The window crew was on a lunch break, and I could hear their laughter floating up from the front yard.

"Howdy," I said.

"There she is," Trish said. She motioned toward her cheek for a kiss, which I delivered.

"I'm finalizing things for tomorrow," Julia said. She still faced her laptop. "It's basically just lunch at this place Daddy liked. And then we can talk about him, I guess? Tell stories or something? Nobody from his South Carolina side can make it. It's going to be so small."

"Where are his . . ." I said.

"The ashes are in a box on the shelf over the washing machine," Trish said.

I joined Julia at the table. The kitchen had a pass-through window, and I watched our mother rinse and slice a tomato. The cabinets had heavy scrollwork and ornate handles. The backsplash was dark-brown vertical tile, at odds with the creamy pebbled pattern of the countertops. The room appeared to have gone through a series of renovations in different decades, and none of them quite aligned.

"Ma," I said. "Are you going to be there tomorrow?"

"If you girls want me to be there, I'll be there." She licked a tomato seed from the side of her hand. "It's up to you."

"Don't do us a *favor*," Julia said. "Go if you want to go."

"Snapping at me isn't going to help."

"She wasn't snapping," I said.

"I don't need it from you either," Trish said. "I was married to your father for fifteen years. Does anyone want to feel sorry for *me* at all?"

"I do," I said. "I do feel sorry for you."

I did not add, because I did not want to fight with my mother, that I felt sorry for her because I remembered that when I was around twelve, she started keeping her high school yearbook on her nightstand. More than once I found her running her fingers over her grainy portrait. *Patricia Annette Walker*, four years before she gave birth to me: feathered hair and blue eyeliner, cross on a thin gold chain. I could not find her name among the lists of superlatives. She belonged to a dance committee, but in the photo she was invisible, standing in the back row. I did not think of her as a person with any secrets until she revealed a hidden bar of white chocolate high on a closet shelf and broke a piece out of the foil for me. For a while after that, I thought that was the only private act of my mother's life, keeping half-melted candy in the same place as her sewing kit.

"I wish you'd brought my grandson," she said, setting the bowl in the center of the table.

"He's going to the Adirondacks with his friend this weekend. He doesn't need to see us all upset anyway."

"Time for plates," Julia said, standing up. "And dressing. And drinks."

"Do I get any thanks for making the salad?" Trish said.

"Thank you," we both said.

Someone was knocking on the front door, saying, "Ma'am, ma'am." He had a question about the windows.

"Goddammit," Julia said. She grabbed a long cardigan off the back of a chair and pulled it on as she went outside.

I got the dressing—thick and too sweet—and the plates. I filled three glasses with water. Trish sat with her elbows on the table, rubbing her hands together. When I sat down, she winced as if I'd touched her.

"How are you doing with all of this, Susan?" she said.

"You mean Dad?"

"Your father. Yes."

"I cried a lot on the train," I said. This wasn't true, but I thought it should have been. My mother and I had spoken right after Julia told us the news—an equal exchange of *I can't believe it* and tense silence.

"Oh, I cried all morning," she said. "I've been doing some real grieving when I'm alone."

"Your face looks pretty good, for having cried all morning."

She frowned at me and pressed lightly on her cheeks.

"I didn't mean *this* morning," she said.

I stared at her, thinking that I should have been able to detect, by her appearance alone, that her first husband had just died. Her hair was freshly trimmed and highlighted. Her shirt, white with pink pinstripes, was wrong for winter. She wore big gold knots in her ears with tiny emeralds in their centers. She smelled like Estée Lauder perfume and baking soda toothpaste. Neither of us touched the salad. I feared that between the two of us there was only uncomfortable sorrow where there should have been, as Trish put it, real grief. We nodded and smiled at two men who passed through the kitchen carrying a new casement window. What do we look like, I wanted to ask as they passed. Do we look sad to you?

Someone Else's Kitchen at Night

The room I was sleeping in was what Julia called her "office"—she had been briefly involved in some multilevel marketing scheme, and there were boxes of spatulas and drinking straws stacked along one wall. The single bed was hard. There was a beadboard bookcase, hip height, filled with Perry's books from engineering school, science fiction (also Perry's), and a box set of Jane Austen novels.

There was a TV from the '90s on the bookcase, and I was surprised to find that it worked. I watched a late-night show, understanding almost none of the celebrity references, and fell asleep on top of the covers. It was three when I woke, thirsty and hot. I could smell the rubber in those boxes of unsold spatulas.

I went to the kitchen for a drink, hoping that Perry had no cause to wander his house in the middle of the night. The light from the stove's digital clock flickered, then went out entirely: Noel was standing in front of it.

"Oh," I said.

"I needed water." He held his glass up to the window as proof.

"Me too," I said.

He got me a glass from the cupboard, filled it, handed it to me.

"You have your own sink upstairs," I said.

"I know."

"Two, in fact."

"I'm familiar with both," he said.

We wore flannel pants, and he wore a white undershirt. I had drawn the hood of my sweatshirt over my head in my sleep, and I felt protected by the cotton against the sides of my face.

"So what are you doing down here?"

"I don't know, Zuzu. Maybe I couldn't find a cup. It's three o'-clock in the morning." He took a noisy sip. "I can't think too clearly at three o'clock in the morning."

"Well, at least we know you aren't thinking about me."

"What's that supposed to mean?"

I hadn't expected to say it. I drank some water. His stomach was slightly rounded, and I could see chest hair through the thin cotton of the shirt. His upper arms were thicker than they'd seemed in the peach-colored button-down.

"You made it very clear in the car that you don't think about me," I said. My glass was empty, and I held it out to him. He set it carefully down in the sink. When he spoke, he kept his back to me.

"I wasn't trying to hurt your feelings," he said.

"You didn't."

"I think I was trying to talk myself into something that maybe wasn't true." He moved the faucet slightly. "I should go back up-stairs."

Unfortunately, I'd seen movies and I'd read books, and I'd gos-siped with other girls during sleepovers, and I knew how it was all supposed to go: He was supposed to profess his love. I was supposed to notice that from this angle, dashed with a bit of moon and the faint blue from the oven's clock, he was, in fact, quite handsome. He was supposed to sink down to his knees on the clean linoleum; per-haps that was the first of the many places we were supposed to fuck. I knew girls who'd had pebbles cast at their windows, or songs re-corded on cassette tapes and dropped through the mail slot. I knew girls who had lifted the welcome mats at their front doors to find that someone had left them a note, a drawing, a flower. I wondered if I was going to go through the rest of my life without flowers or pebbles or confessions, if this—Noel Rafferty awkwardly drinking water in my sister's kitchen—was the most I could hope for.

"Goodnight, Noel," I said. I left him standing at the sink.

In Julia's guest room, I felt a rush of joy at the sight of a new mes-sage from Cash.

> CASH: so we have a problem
> ZUZU: YOU have problems
> CASH: ok well

CASH: our furnace is fucked and can't be fixed until
after long weekend
CASH: so this is not a comfortable place to stay
ZUZU: are you making this up to avoid me
CASH: . . .
CASH: you are paranoid
CASH: P&M are going to my in-laws but I'm staying
in the city
CASH: let's meet here instead

I CLICKED THE link: a boutique hotel in Beacon Hill with a famous bar. The cream-colored rooms, each with a fireplace, filled me with the kind of longing I usually felt for what I thought of as the happiest times, though I was certain I'd never been there.

The Gathering

J ulia's email invitation did not refer to a memorial; rather, people were invited to a "gathering." It was a tavern lunch, with meat loaf and a salad bar, the kind of place where you could still smoke inside. Julia said that Dad had liked the bartenders and loved the Buffalo wings. Some of our father's friends from the Vineyard era of his life showed up, four white men in jeans with acoustic guitars. They started and abandoned a number of Neil Young songs at a corner table. One of them kept wiping his eyes with a paper napkin, then tucking the napkin back into his shirt like a pocket square. Although Julia had requested that I come early to help her, my "help" was mostly sitting at her side, agreeing with her on details. Our father, for instance, had hated Caesar salad; in his honor, it was taken off the menu for the afternoon.

The room was dim, and when I glanced up at the lamps I saw that they were thick with dust. Agnes, who had driven from our house, arrived even earlier than Julia and me; she was sitting in our car, dealing with work emails, when my sister and I pulled up. The sight of my wife, dressed in her court clothes, made me start to cry. She held me for a solid minute, in complete silence, before we went inside.

During the lunch, she shifted into what I thought of as her professional mode, talking to Perry about her work, occasionally letting him talk about his. I wanted no part of that; truthfully, I wanted no part of any of it. I was tired and hungry and I didn't want the tavern's greasy food. Heidi was a good cook, according to Agnes, and I knew that while we were there I would mostly be left alone, in deference to my grief. I looked forward to getting on the road.

Someone touched my shoulder: Gary, one of the guitar players. He was unsteady on his feet.

"You and your sister turned out beautiful," he said.

"Thank you."

"I'm sure Dennis was proud."

"Yes," I said. Julia came to stand beside me, and he touched her shoulder and said the same thing to her. Then he asked if either of us had checked on our mother.

"Mom's not here," Julia said.

"She's out in the parking lot," Gary said, tapping lightly on one of the windows.

I didn't believe him, but I peered through the dirty glass. Trish was idling in a clearly marked loading zone.

"There she is," I said.

MY SISTER AND I walked out together. When Trish saw us, she un-locked her car doors.

"You can't park here," Julia said, taking the front seat. She kissed our mother's cheek.

"Actually," Trish said, "you can park wherever you please at your husband's funeral."

"*Husband*?" I said. "*Funeral*?"

"You know what I mean."

Our mother's appearance, as ever, fell short of beauty but sug-gested plenty of effort. Under her quilted jacket she wore a gray tur-tleneck with a tasseled drawstring at the waist and a pleated skirt. She had repaired the runs in her stockings with nail polish—I could see the clear lacquer when I leaned forward between the front seats—and her shoes, with squared toes, had brassy buckles on their sides.

"Anyone want to feel sorry for *me* today? Anyone? I was married to that man in there for a long time, you know."

"He's not in there, Mom," I said.

"You know what I mean."

"Also, you did that bit at Julia's house yesterday."

She frowned.

"It's not a 'bit.'"

"Come in and have a drink," Julia said.

"I'll join you in a minute," I said.

Once they were gone, I let myself stretch all the way across the back seat. The sky through the sunroof was gray and flat, as bored with me as I was with it. I took a photo and sent it to Cash: my view. When I sat up and looked out the back windshield, I saw Noel in the parking lot, carrying a massive arrangement of orchids. I knocked on the glass to get his attention, but he didn't notice. I opened the door and got out of the car, hurrying after him.

"Noel," I said.

"Zuzu." He shifted so that the flowers weren't in front of his face. "I'm not coming in, I just wanted to drop these off for you guys."

"That was nice of you. You want a drink or something?"

He looked down at himself. "I don't want to go in dressed like this."

"There are like fifty old men in there wearing jeans."

"I don't want to impose, or intrude, or whatever. I just wanted to drop off some flowers."

"Okay," I said. "Well, you can put them down for a minute. I don't want to go back in there yet."

Noel hesitated, then set the orchids by my feet.

"I know I said it the other day, but I really am sorry about your dad. I think he yelled at me once for throwing a snowball during pickup at school."

"Ha. Sounds like him."

"Also, you know that monologue you did senior year?"

"Kind of, yeah."

"He cried during it."

I pulled my skirt tighter over my legs.

"How do you know?"

"Because he asked my mom for a tissue, and she told me about it later. Marilyn Rafferty loves her gossip."

It was not the crying that got to me—I had seen my father cry. He was quick to weep at sentimental movies; he wiped his eyes when he described the moments his girls were born. It was Noel's mother's name that startled me. I hadn't thought of Marilyn Rafferty a single time since I finished high school. I could still picture her in high-waisted plaid pants, handing out a plastic-wrapped slice of her chocolate zucchini cake at a bake sale, her glasses askew on her nose. She liked us all to call her Miss Marilyn. She was alive, and Noel could mention her casually and then carry on with his day. Every time I said *Dennis Braeburn* now, it meant something else.

"You okay?" Noel said.

"I'd just picked out a coat for him," I said. "A raincoat. I guess he needed one."

Noel nodded.

"But I didn't bring it to him. Even though I probably should have."

"Zuzu."

"Too late now." He stood there with me for a minute, while I felt both the pointlessness and the truth of what I'd said.

THE TAVERN WAS almost empty when I went back inside. Perry was leaning on the bar, talking about sports with the bartender. I poked his arm.

"Hey," I said.

"Hey, Zuzu."

"I just wanted to ask, like, how you think she's doing."

He straightened up. His shaved head was golden brown under the light.

"Julia's doing all right," he said, crossing his arms over his chest. I sensed that he didn't trust me. His eyes flicked toward the ladies' room, then back to me. "And yourself?"

"Fine."

"Hmm."

"Not *fine*. Sad. But getting used to it, I guess."

"I don't know," he said, looking up at the scalloped glass of a hanging lamp, "if I will ever get used to not having Dennis around. He was a funny man."

Julia came out of the ladies' room.

"Whenever I drink ginger ale, this baby won't stop kicking." She leaned against Perry, who wrapped her in his arms and placed both of his hands on her stomach. He looked like he could have easily swept her over one shoulder. No one had ever touched me like that, with protectiveness and pride; or, if Agnes had, it didn't look the same. She was only two inches taller than I was.

"You okay?" Julia said, looking at me.

"Yeah. Yeah."

"You can get going. It's just us left."

"I should get you home," Perry said, resting his chin on her head. "Mama needs her sleep."

"Where's Agnes?"

"Out in the car," I said. "Work stuff."

Julia reached for me and I leaned toward her. Her hair smelled like tropical fruit. She rubbed a small circle on my back and took a deep breath. I braced for a confession, or maybe something about our father, but she made her voice gravelly and deep and said, "You girls turned out beautiful," imitating Gary, and then she laughed.

Why Didn't She Just Marry Heidi

On the drive to Heidi's, we stopped at Dunkin' Donuts for decaf coffees. Merging onto the turnpike, Agnes took my hand.

At a tollbooth, I was ready for our usual argument—it annoyed her that I didn't have express lane windshield tags—but I just handed her the exact change and dropped my wallet down by my feet, on a pile of unopened mail she'd left there, and neither of us mentioned it.

In the Stop & Shop parking lot, phone to her ear, Agnes grabbed a piece of our mail and a pen. She wrote *grapefruit juice, detergent, blueberries (x4)*. When she said, "You don't need to do that," I knew Heidi had offered to pay her back. I stared at the list.

"What are all those blueberries for?"

"A pie, probably," Agnes said, unbuckling her seat belt. She didn't ask me if I wanted anything from the store. She strode with purpose, her bag knocking lightly against her hip. She looked like a woman running an errand for her wife. I checked my phone: nothing from Cash.

Why hadn't she just married Heidi?

I used to tease her about this, back when we could abide more teasing. She always said, *We were too young*, even though Heidi, who had been a grad student when they met, was seven years older than Agnes. *We were too young*, as if she and I had been well into middle age when we went to the Ashworth City Hall. In fact, we'd been twenty-seven. I have long wished we had a romantic story to tell, but ours was a practical conversation. I'd been sweeping the apartment, and when I mentioned marriage to Agnes, I was on my knees with a dustpan.

Later I would think, *At least I was on my knees.*

There was already tension between us that summer, in part because she never swept the floor and I always did. I made note of this often, so that when I showed her the dustpan and its cache of crumbs, she took it as the criticism it was meant to be. She had done the near impossible, securing a post as a summer associate at a top firm—these spots were largely reserved for 2Ls—and when she told me she didn't have time to sweep, it was almost true. Her long workdays were followed by summer associate programming. She went to wine tastings, Broadway shows. She made soup dumplings, she went to galleries after hours. The firm dazzled their summers, dipping them, over and over, into the riches of the life they could afford if they came back after they graduated. Agnes and I agreed that it was excessive, but over time she complained less and sent more proof of her spoils. I would receive, midday, photos of lobster tail poached in tomato broth, or pastel macarons at high tea. Partners would praise her in emails, which she would screenshot and send to me.

It was, of course, exactly what we wanted. It was the entire reason we'd met, back when we were prospective law students. It was the reason we read numbingly boring textbooks, so that we could be prepared for the occasional cold call in class, and so that we could do well on our exams.

I had no real reputation, unlike Agnes, who was widely admired. I was a middle-of-the-pack student. I hadn't dropped out after losing ten pounds in three weeks, the way one classmate had; I hadn't started pulling out my own hair, like someone on law review, who had then famously been persuaded to take a leave of absence. I was fine. I was keeping my head above water.

While Agnes ate lobster and went to wine tastings, I worked as a research assistant for a professor whose position at the university was largely a formality. I had no free tickets to shows, no soup dumpling classes. I usually brought a bagel into the law library, where I wasn't supposed to have food at all, and where I spent most of the time cite-checking articles my professor was working on. The work was silent, repetitive, and far from lucrative. I didn't love it, but I also didn't mind it, which was how I figured work was supposed to be. I did not believe work should be the centerpiece of my life.

As I worked I saw the mechanics of law and policy, their perfect design, their absolute logic, and the way human beings failed to make it work. Or I saw laws that were perfect only in their cruelty. The professor I worked for was writing a book on miscegenation laws—an academic tome that roughly twenty people would ever read—but each time I sat down to cite-check, I felt a deepening bitterness, along with an increasing desire to claim whatever rights could be mine. We had to marry, I said, because we could.

"Listen to you," she said. "You wouldn't even go to the Pride parade with me."

"That's because I don't like crowds," I said.

WHY DIDN'T SHE just marry Heidi?

Heidi didn't ask her. I did. I asked her with a dustpan in my hand.

RIGHT AFTER SPRING finals our 2L year, Agnes and I went to Ashworth City Hall. We wore vintage-shop white cotton dresses that we planned to dye different colors later on, to prove how practical we were. We never dyed them. Later, we admitted that neither of us wanted to.

Rosewood

S plit-rail fences lined Heidi's driveway. Her house, Rosewood Cottage, was the kind of place I would have rented for a long weekend with a lover, if I'd had that kind of life. Rosewood didn't actually belong to her, but she'd been in it for so many years that it had lost its formal name on campus. The students, including the ones who lived in Rosewood Dorm, just called it Heidi's. She had explained this to me, not without pride, on our last visit.

There were no students in sight when we parked behind Heidi's Prius. As soon as I got out of the car, her blue-eyed husky bounded over and jumped on me, and I fell in mud and slush.

"Sorry," Heidi said. "He's just excited to see you." She'd stopped dyeing and cutting her hair since the last time I'd seen her; it was long and brown, and she'd tucked the ends into her funnel-neck sweater. Both her sweater and her jeans were red. She made a kind of apologetic bow but didn't offer to help me up. Agnes seemed momentarily confused, an overnight bag in each hand, but then she shifted both bags into her right hand and offered me her left, pulling me upright, it felt, without much effort from me at all.

The dog had distracted Heidi from the perfunctory condolences she delivered as we filed through her front door: She was sorry for my loss, was there anything she could do. No, I said, but thank you.

LATER, FROM AN unfamiliar bed, I would consider the many times my wife may have decided to sleep with Heidi. It might have been right then, when I sat in the muddy slush in my black wool, the blue-eyed husky sniffing my shoes. Maybe when she opened Heidi's fridge and saw a piecrust made from scratch. Perhaps it was the aggressive wholesomeness of Heidi's house, the Castile soap and the kale chips, the wool blankets, the taste of the well water, the omnipresence of the dog. Maybe I should have paid more attention when they were both humming a song I didn't know, and I had to ask what it was, and Agnes started laughing and didn't explain what was funny.

Perhaps it had to do with the lump, the lump that none of us were talking about.

Perhaps my wife was enchanted by Lake Placid, a tennis court that Heidi had flooded in deep winter so that it froze into a skating rink. Heidi had extra hockey skates and offered me a pair, holding them up by their knotted laces. I told her I didn't know how.

"I thought all New Englanders knew how to ice-skate," she said.

"I'll stay here and have a cup of tea, if that's all right." I'd changed out of my dress and into thermal pants and Agnes's gray sweatshirt—

I didn't care what I looked like in front of Heidi—but I hadn't changed my underwear, and hadn't realized that it, too, was damp and cold from my fall outside.

"There's tons of tea," Heidi said, winding a scarf around her neck. "Let me know if you need help finding anything."

THE KETTLE HAD so much grease spattered on the enamel that I gave it a quick scrub, then changed my mind. I didn't actually want tea; it had just sounded like a good excuse for staying inside. The windows over the sink gave onto a perfect view of Lake Placid, and I watched them skate, admiring the ease with which Agnes raised her arms and twirled. I'd forgotten that she was actually quite good at this; it wasn't something we did together, because I hadn't bothered to learn how.

Another thought I had, watching them skate: Why weren't they touching? Why, even when Heidi fell hard on her knees, were they keeping at least eight feet between them?

"Help her up, would you?" I said. The dog flicked its tail and my breath clouded the glass. I watched them take off their skates and trudge back from the tennis court, Agnes far ahead of Heidi, as if they didn't want to be seen together. Agnes came in first, dropping her coat and hat on the floor, just like she did at home.

"There's my favorite wife," she said.

I pointed at the coat and hat, the wet boots lying on their sides.

"You're going to leave that there?"

Heidi looked up from unzipping her vest.

"I don't mind," she said.

I texted Cash: I should have learned how to ice skate.

> CASH: ???
> ZUZU: I'm staying right next to an ice rink
> CASH: where are you
> ZUZU: 25 min from your house

Nothing from Cash after that.

Heidi served white bean and sage soup, a green salad with matchsticks of apple in it, anadama bread, and blueberry pie. I admired the ceramic pie dish, and she told us she'd bought it at the annual faculty yard sale.

"We should have a yard sale," I said.

"You sound a little congested," Heidi said.

"Don't start with the yard sale bit," Agnes said.

Heidi looked at her.

"What's the yard sale bit?"

"We have a storage unit." Agnes took a piece of piecrust from my plate and ate it. "And I just don't have time to deal with it."

"I've told her I'd do it myself," I said.

"Ha. If I let you do it yourself, you'd just throw everything out."

"I'm sick of paying for it," I said.

"I can't deal with it right now."

"Okay, but we can't just rent that thing forever."

"She's a busy lady," Heidi said.

Perhaps Agnes decided right then, or while they were sitting on the couch after dinner. When I offered to do the dishes they both accepted without a gesture of hesitation. The husky trotted over to sit by my feet, wagging his tail, whining occasionally.

"Is he bothering you?" Heidi called.

I told her he wasn't, though in fact the dog, who was clearly used to receiving food scraps if he sat by the sink, kept whining and nosing me. I was lying, and I was sure that Agnes could tell.

BY THE TIME Heidi was brushing her teeth upstairs, there had still been no mention of the lump.

I asked Agnes if it had come up while they were skating.

"Nope," she said, shaking out the top sheet. We were making up the futon in the living room.

"Are you going to ask her about it?"

Agnes handed me a pillowcase.

"It's not for me to ask about."

"But isn't that kind of why we're here?"

Agnes yawned and flipped her head over, shaking more volume

into her hair. She got into bed with her back to me and started scrolling on her phone, and I fed my pillow into its case and got in on my side, coughing.

"This thing is hard," I said, thumping the mattress.

No response.

Other things that elicited no response from Agnes: when I put my hand on her hip; when I coughed so hard that I gagged; when, halfway to sleep myself, I whispered her name and asked if she was still awake.

I HAD A dream about Heidi's breasts. She asked me to feel them and I did, reluctantly, while Agnes watched from a rocking chair. The breasts split open in my hands and crystal prisms fell out. I kept saying, *Unfortunately I feel something here, I feel something here.*

Someone Else's Kitchen at Night Again

Around four in the morning, I woke myself up coughing. I woke Heidi up as well, and she came downstairs in a blue pajama set. I was surprised to see that she slept with some kind of mask on her cheekbones. We both crept past Agnes, who was snoring on her back.

In the kitchen, Heidi turned on the kettle.

"You still have both lungs?" she said.

"For now." I coughed into my sleeve. "You know, this is the second time this week I've been standing in a kitchen late at night with someone other than Agnes."

"What does that mean?"

"I mean, literally, I was in my sister's kitchen last night."

She looked at me for so long that I feared I had misspoken.

"Valerian root?"

"Okay," I said. I sat down at the table where we'd eaten, a table I had wiped clean. She took two mugs off the drying rack. I hoped she was planning to take hers back up to bed, but she pulled out the chair across from me. Without her pink-purple hair she had less grandeur. I noticed that her nose was rather long, her nostrils small, her eyes a shade close together.

"Thanks for bringing Agnes," she said.

"Couldn't have stopped her if I wanted to."

"That's true." Heidi got up to turn off the kettle, and then she proceeded to praise Agnes in a way that I understood was meant to flatter me. People loved to compliment me by saying nice things about Agnes, and in the early years of our marriage, I had been happy to collect the scattered valentines on her behalf. I'd chosen well, and I'd been lucky to be chosen. Agnes was a go-getter, a fire-cracker. The subtext often seemed to be this: You, Zuzu, are none of these things, but you get to sleep with someone who is. You get to make coffee for her and wash her clothes, which she has every right to leave heaped on the floor next to her side of the bed, because she doesn't have time to deal with it, and you do.

I had several coughing fits during Heidi's lecture on Agnes. When I finally stopped, she told me she was going to run a hot shower, and that she wanted me to sit in the steam.

"Aren't *we* supposed to be taking care of *you*?" I said.

She wound the string of the tea bag around the bag itself, wring-ing tiny drops into her mug.

"Do you remember the first time the three of us hung out to-gether?" she said.

"Yes. That place in the West Village. It's not there anymore."

"You flirted with the bartender all night."

"Yeah, probably." I shrugged.

"The bartender was this huge guy with a pierced tongue?"

"I mostly remember how clear it was that you didn't like me."

"Why should I have liked you? You were flirting with the bartender. I didn't know how much of a habit that was for you. And, you know, it just gets harder and harder to change, the older you get."

"Oh my God." I laughed. "I get it. You didn't approve. Maybe you still don't."

"My opinion has no weight anymore." She winked at me, but it was a mirthless wink.

"You realize she let me read that email you sent," I said.

"What email."

"You said I didn't seem trustworthy, that I seemed *really* into the bartender, and that I struck you as someone who was 'claiming to be bi just to be interesting.' You also said you bet her five thousand bucks that I'd suggest we open our relationship within the first five years."

Heidi maintained eye contact while she sipped her tea.

"You're not denying it," I said.

"Why would I?" She shrugged. "I wrote it. I didn't know you would memorize it."

I had read it while I sat on Agnes's lap. She kept pinching my sides, trying to distract me. *Who cares what Heidi wrote*, she'd said, biting my shoulder. *Heidi's thoughts are immaterial.*

"Well, in spite of your warnings, she still wanted me. And here we are." I thumped my chest. Heidi watched, not without sympathy, as I suffered another coughing fit.

"You need steam," she said.

I followed her upstairs and sat obediently on the edge of the tub while she turned on the tap. The shower curtain had sunflowers on it and smelled faintly of mold. There were three toothbrushes in a jelly jar on the sink, and none of them looked clean. I didn't like the taste of the valerian root. Knowing she had no choice but to nod politely, I showed her a dozen photos of Reid and Gideon in the Adirondacks: sledding, jumping over a stream, adding more whipped cream to their hot chocolate.

"You're right," she said, shifting her eyes to the running water. "Agnes wanted you. And you wanted her more than I gave you credit for."

"What does that mean?"

"It means you're still here," she said. She tapped the edge of my mug. "Seriously, drink this, it'll help you get back to sleep."

"Is this the poison in a fairy tale?"

"Is this"—she paused to shake her sunflower-patterned shower curtain on its rings—"a fairy tale setting?"

"Probably not," I said.

"Sleep well," Heidi said.

The Search

I don't know how long I sat there. Long enough to watch water bead on the iron door latches, long enough to need to wipe the mirror before I could see my face. I wore a crown of frizz. I looked humbled by the steam, softened and rumpled. My exile had not been flattering.

When I opened the door, the hallway was cold and dark, imprinted faintly with dog. I went downstairs and climbed back into bed, and several minutes passed before I realized I was alone. Usually, Agnes shoved my foot away from her when it drifted to her side—even in sleep, she could shove—but I swung my leg all the way across the cool sheet, and nothing happened to me.

It seemed impossible that we could have passed each other on the stairs without noticing, but I harbored this hope for a while. I listened for water in the pipes. I lost patience with the silence and went into the kitchen, where nothing had moved since Heidi made the tea and I made an allusion to the lump.

I looked in the pantry, where, tucked in among the cans of beans and tomatoes, I saw an unopened twenty-five-dollar pouch of matcha powder. This irritated me, possibly because it was the kind of thing Agnes would buy and never use. I looked in the little coat closet and counted three pairs of Wellington boots: same brand, same size, different colors. Excess, dressed up as Yankee frugality.

My wife, of course, was not in the pantry, nor was she in the closet.

Perhaps it had occurred to Agnes that we'd never in our lives played hide-and-seek together, and she'd woken up feeling inspired to start the game. Perhaps she could fit under the futon; I checked by the light of my phone. It was physically impossible for an adult to slip under there. I lifted the lid of the steamer trunk in the living room, expecting heirloom family quilts or some other Heidi-ish bullshit, and was thrilled to see a video-game console—I couldn't have said what kind—and plastic cases of what I assumed were video games, with thunderbolts and caped men on them, presumably heaped into the trunk so we wouldn't see them.

Knowing I would find nothing of use, I pushed on the door that opened directly into the empty dormitory. I walked the length of one hall, using my phone as a flashlight, stumbling over an ice hockey stick that someone had left on the floor. The bulletin board had a single notice on it for choir tryouts.

One more time: under the futon, inside the closet, inside the pantry.

I sent Agnes a text—Where are you?—without expecting a response.

One more time: hold breath, listen for water in the pipes. Occasionally, Agnes woke up so hot that she showered to cool down, though that was mostly during the summer months. I went upstairs just long enough to see that the bathroom was empty.

It occurred to me that she might have gone to sleep in the car—she had done that once before, when we'd gone camping (her idea), and I'd been "thrashing around" inside the tent.

In the car, I idled outside Rosewood Cottage, the gray sweatshirt and thermal pants both damp from the steam. I'd slid my feet into the same black heels I'd taken off when I arrived. My wallet was still on the floor in front of the passenger seat, along with the unopened mail. I picked up an envelope from the storage unit in Jersey City: in red block letters, it said FINAL NOTICE across the flap. We had thirty days to collect our belongings before the building was razed. According to the letter, they had tried notifying Agnes, the account holder, by both email and phone.

"Ha," I said, alone in the car. "Finally." I took a photo of the letter and sent it to Agnes, a task so mundane that for a moment, waiting for the attachment to upload, I felt normal. I listened to the sound the text made as I sent it. That feeling I'd had in the gazebo—that yearning to swim in the Hudson River until I was lost—came thundering back to me.

I pressed the horn, watching Heidi's bedroom window. I did it again, the noise so loud that it frightened me. There were other faculty in the nearby dorms, families with young children. One house still had its Christmas tree up, with blue lights set to flicker on and off, the same kind my mother used to buy. It was the thought of a three a.m. confrontation with Heidi's blue-tree neighbors that sent me driving down the unlit road, skidding a bit on the ice, hurrying for the exit through the always-open gates, wondering if there were any other possible interpretation of events, if I had gone crazy, if perhaps my wife had really disappeared, and if in a few hours Heidi would call, looking for both of us.

Where Are You

Heidi didn't call. I spent some time in the food court of a twenty-four-hour rest area off I-95. A man in a green uniform was mopping the floors, and we exchanged a nod. The place was technically open, but there were metal grates pulled down in front of the restaurant counters; only the convenience mart was available. I bought a travel-size bottle of mouthwash, a cup of burned coffee, a bag of greasy-looking sunflower seeds. I was aware that I appeared to be significantly down on my luck: the hair, made unkempt by the steam; the thermal pants worn with heels. I ate the sunflower seeds and drank the coffee until my stomach hurt.

Around six, when Agnes finally called, I let it go straight to voicemail.

Her message, in its entirety: "Zuzu? Where the fuck are you?"

Her second message: "I assume you just went for a drive or something. Can you please confirm you're okay?"

Oh, Agnes, your third message—from your own phone number, no less. "Zuzu, this is Heidi. Agnes is worried about you. Could you give her a call?"

HEIDI HAD A white iron headboard, and I could see my wife's hands gripping it. I could see the rose-gold bracelet she rarely took off. I saw the tendons in her throat when she threw her head back. Picturing this scene, I felt oddly calm; there was neither desire nor jealousy. There was only the general discomfort one feels when one has been deceived.

Or—I was willing to concede this, alone in the car—I was being ridiculous. Perhaps Agnes had gone for a walk in the brisk night air. Perhaps she was keeping her distance because she was afraid of catching my cough. Perhaps Heidi had finally broken down about her lump and sought quiet consolation from my wife.

> ZUZU: hellooo???
>
> AGNES: where are you
>
> ZUZU: where were you
>
> ZUZU: I couldn't find you anywhere at Heidi's
>
> ZUZU: the only place I didn't look was in her room
>
> AGNES: never went in her room
>
> ZUZU: literally the only possible explanation
>
> AGNES: no

I sat for a while, waiting, as if I didn't know her well enough to understand her comfort with silence. Silence was her instinct when she was upset, her cool retreat and her tool for punishment. Several minutes passed before she wrote again.

AGNES: I think you were looking for any excuse to leave

ZUZU: I wouldn't have come in the first place if all I wanted to do was leave

Security

I went back into the convenience mart a final time, for orange juice and a packaged donut with chocolate glaze. The combination gave me terrible heartburn, but I ate and drank anyway, then texted Cash: Are you still @ hotel? I can stop by in the afternoon.

He wrote back within a minute: Still here.

I wanted to give the impression that I had things to do—that I was not, in fact, idling next to a gas station off a major highway, intermittently fighting with my wife over text. I had left my overnight bag at Heidi's, and I needed some clothes. I feared that the hotel in Beacon Hill would escort me out of the lobby at the sight of my heels-and-sweatpants combination. I found a mall not far from the rest area, and drove there with the windows down, hoping it would somehow improve my increasingly matted hair. It did not.

As THE GLASS doors parted, I worried that I looked like I couldn't afford anything in the department store. I found the ladies' lounge and rinsed with mouthwash, and then I bought clothes without trying them on. I chose a brand of jeans I'd heard of but never worn—Agnes and I considered them prohibitively expensive—and a long gray wrap sweater that tied on the side, with a black silk camisole that was slightly too tight underneath. I found a wool fedora that smelled faintly of the hair spray someone else must have been wearing when she tried it on.

As was my habit, I wondered how many minutes of work it had taken Agnes to earn the money I was about to spend. It was a habit I'd formed years ago, when I first started caring for Gideon full-time while she went back to the firm. I had anticipated exhaustion. I had anticipated that one of us would sleep in on Saturdays, and the other on Sundays. I had not anticipated that she would claim both mornings for herself because she believed that I could nap whenever the baby napped. I had not anticipated that this chasm would widen and deepen every Saturday, every Sunday, without exception. I didn't know about the way resentment could build up, how thick and water resistant it could become, how it left its greasy slick on everything, until it was the dominant flavor of everything we ate.

PLACING THE HAT in an old-fashioned box, the cashier praised the way the brim flattered my face and told me I had excellent cheekbones. The security guard she'd been chatting with nodded in agreement.

"She really does," he said. Then, turning to me: "You really do."

"Thank you," I said. He had a graying mustache and he wore pleasant, if excessive, cologne. I looked at the cashier and willed her to finish wrapping my clothes in tissue paper so that I could unwrap them and put them on.

"What are you doing over here, anyway, Charles," the cashier said.

"Just my job, Jamie."

"Here we go." She rolled her eyes and took a quick sip of the coffee she'd hidden behind the counter.

"Actually, this question is for you too," Charles said, looking at me. "For the lovely lady who just bought the hat."

"I'm in a hurry this morning," I said, but the transaction had come to a halt. Charles was, in fact, doing his job: He wanted to know if either of us had seen someone in a neon-yellow T-shirt, carrying two canvas totes that were apparently full of stolen shoes. Charles's walkie-talkie crackled, and he silenced it with a slap to one of its buttons.

"I haven't seen anybody," Jamie said. She wrapped my sweater, placed it in the bag, and printed my receipt. "She's my first customer today." They both looked at me.

"I haven't seen anybody either," I said.

He looked at his hands, and my hands, and Jamie's hands.

"One of us does this and we all look bad," he said.

Jamie made a sound of agreement and turned to tend to the

register. Charles stayed there, waiting for me to respond. I hoisted the bags off the counter.

"I don't think I know what you mean," I said. "Have a nice day."

I KNEW EXACTLY what he meant. I tried to ignore it while I checked my texts and email—nothing from Agnes—and while I bought new boots: Italian, black, requiring great patience and concentration to tie. Changing in a narrow stall, the discomfort of my new lace underwear shocked me. The jeans were stiff and hard to zip, and I spent several minutes trying to position the hat so that it wouldn't look too affected. When I came out, I tripped and dropped my bag onto the carpet. Charles the security guard was there to pick it up, as if he'd been waiting for me.

"You again," he said. My wallet had opened, and some coins had scattered, along with the envelope from the storage unit. He picked it up and read from the list Agnes had written on the flap: "Grapefruit juice, detergent, blueberries times four." His knees cracked when he stood. "You're not in the right place for grapefruit juice and blueberries, you know."

"That's an old list." I pulled it from his hand.

"You're in a rush?"

"Yes."

He looked at me, half smiling, waiting for me to respond. For the first time since I'd driven through that campus gate, I missed Agnes. Even when strangers couldn't tell that she and I were a couple, they were less likely to assume familiarity with me if she was at my side. They were less likely to look at my skin and say, for instance, *One of us does this and we all look bad.*

His walkie-talkie crackled and he turned his head, preparing to speak into it.

"Good luck," he said.

Lobby

I n the lobby of Cash's hotel, a toddler dropped a cup of grapes all over the marble floor and started trying to climb one of the potted trees by the reception desk. I felt an urge to help the mother, an instant solidarity that I recalled from the first years of Gideon's life, when women opened doors for me, lifted one end of the stroller, found fallen teething rings.

I sank to my knees, feeling the new jeans bite into me. "Here," I said, "let me help," collecting the grapes within my reach. The mother turned, and for a moment I was so sure that she was Molly Pierce-Cashel—the hazel eyes, the hair an artful tangle of blond curls anchored by an invisible clip, the expensive trench coat, the faint soapy odor—that I stood up quickly and backed away, crushing the grapes in my hand. "I didn't know you'd be here," I said, looking at Portia, who was not Portia, and who had given up her tree climbing to grab her mother's leg. Her mother—whoever she was, she wasn't Molly Pierce-Cashel—asked me if we'd met before.

"Sorry, no," I said. "I thought you were someone else."

She lifted her daughter into her arms and approached the reception desk, and I stepped outside, shaking bits of grape onto the sidewalk. Believing, for two or three seconds, that I was standing before Cash's wife, I had felt terrible disappointment, as if I'd lost a great opportunity.

Outage

May 8, 2004

A few nights before graduation, Cash helped me pack up my room. I had both of my windows open and two box fans set to high, but it was still miserably hot. We shared the lone can of beer I'd found in the fridge. He'd brought music, and even though my CD player was already in a box, he cut through the tape and freed it from the towel I'd wrapped it in. He put on a mix, then filled another box with books.

"I was going to sell those," I said.

"All of them?" He pulled out *The Age of Innocence*. "Even this?"

"Why, did you want to keep that one?"

"Maybe." He flipped through it, then dropped it back in with the others. "I'm starting to realize, like, if I didn't read it in college, I'm never going to read it."

"You can still read, Cash. You're not going to lose the ability." I was on my hands and knees, rolling up the rug. "Can you help with this?"

"Don't do that yet."

"It's the last thing left."

"Don't," he said. "You kept getting splinters in here, remember?" He grabbed one of my feet and held it until I pretended to kick him.

"You should come on the camping trip after graduation," he said.

"I don't have any camping stuff." He was unfolding the flaps of a closed box. "Cash, stop. You're *unpacking*."

He pulled the cap off a bottle of perfume and sprayed it into the air.

"Cash. Put it back."

"Okay, okay. Calm down." He wrapped the bottle back in its newspaper. "I have an extra camping pad."

"I don't even know what that is."

"You can share with me, I have enough stuff."

"I don't feel like driving up there."

"Vermont's not that far." He tied a pair of my sneakers together by their laces. "Molly said she won't go either, if you don't go."

The lights flickered and went out. The CD player cut off and the fans gave up their quiet roar, the blades turning slowly until they were still. We did not touch each other. In the hot, dark room I felt a surge of dread: What if I had the kind of life where the lights went out and nothing happened, and then they went back on and nothing happened.

One of my housemates shouted that she had a flashlight; a minute later, power returned. I took the disc out and handed it to Cash, and he left while I was wrapping the CD player back in its towel.

He wasn't always rescuing me, bringing me dinner and driving me places, making sure I didn't get splinters. He did those things, and sometimes I took care of him. Sometimes I made him tea. Once, I heard him insist that he didn't need to move his Jeep to the other side of the street to avoid a ticket, and I knew he was wrong. I waited until he was in the shower, and then I took his keys and moved the car myself, knowing by the time he realized it he would feel only relief.

Embers

⌐ꜱ

May 15, 2004

olly had to show me how to light the camping stove. I was scrambling eggs and refried beans in a cast-iron skillet, then scooping a spoonful into the tortillas she was warming over the fire. Each burrito she rolled looked exactly the same. I asked her if she'd had professional training.

"Who, me?" She was wrapping each burrito in foil, then placing it on the edge of the fire pit to keep it warm.

"Yeah, like a summer job or something."

Cash was sitting on the cooler, watching Molly's boyfriend, Hugh, tune his guitar.

"Ha," Cash said, without looking away from the instrument. "Molly Pierce with a summer job."

"Shut up." She rolled a scrap of foil into a tiny ball and threw it at him. "I did house-sitting."

"For your own parents. At their lake house."

"Zuzu!" Molly said. "Make him stop."

Hugh and Cash, absorbed by the guitar, didn't even glance over. There were fifteen of us at the site, a cluster of fleece jackets reeking of smoke. Everywhere I looked I saw another thirty-two-ounce water bottle covered in bumper stickers. There were bumper stickers all over everyone's hand-me-down Volvos and Saabs. Julia teased me for months when I worried aloud that my car was "too shiny." I didn't know how to explain it to her.

"I can't make him do anything, Molly," I said.

WE TOOK A hike at night—Molly brought extra headlamps—and once I stopped looking for the glimmer of animal eyes, I began to enjoy the sound of the crickets and our out-of-sync breathing. Each footfall was so soft it hardly happened; we could just as easily have been walking above the ground. I gulped the wet pine and moss air. I loved it, and regretted, again, how many precious hours I spent at the mall.

When we turned to head back to our site, Cash held me by the elbow and asked me to wait with him. Within thirty seconds, we could neither see nor hear our friends.

"We need more kindling," he said. "Will you help?"

"Can you promise that I'm not going to get attacked by a fisher cat?"

He laughed and knelt by me, choosing from the scattered sticks and fallen branches.

"What do you know about fisher cats?"

"You gave me a very long, boring lecture once about fisher cats and porcupines. How the fisher cat jumps around until it tires the porcupine out. Also, how they aren't really cats."

He turned his headlamp off and kissed me, and his forehead pressed the switch on my lamp. It was suddenly dark, and I reached for him mostly out of fear and surprise. He was already reaching for me.

We kissed again, and then he said we should bring back the kindling. My mind wandered into the mess of the logistics—I could tell we were going to sleep together, but I wasn't sure where, and I didn't want it to be outside. I harbored a "somewhat excessive" (Cash's words) fear of poison ivy; I had seen someone's leg swell to three times its size with a poison ivy rash, and she'd worn a short dress to a dance anyway.

We dropped off kindling and went straight into his five-person tent, a good thirty yards from the fire pit, surrounded by trees. I hadn't brought a reusable water bottle with me, just the plastic kind from a vending machine, so I took sips from his metal canteen. The water tasted slightly grainy, like it was from a rocky spring. His water, I decided, was better than other water. His sleeping bag, already unrolled in one corner, smelled like sun and dirt. The zipper, surprisingly cold, bit into my back.

The previous year, when I'd slept with him while my eardrum burned, I had wished for more noise from him. I wanted a sound to trap and replay privately. It was better in the tent, frantic and silent, the silence a necessary part of our being together; it felt like a joint project, our silence. He sounded, when he breathed, like he needed more air. I kissed the skin around his eyes, to remind him of what I wanted.

OUTSIDE, MOLLY'S BOYFRIEND, Hugh, was playing his guitar. Our friends were roasting marshmallows, debating whether to toast them lightly or set them on fire. Cash pulled his pants up and buckled his belt and went back out, and I dressed and lingered inside the tent, wondering what people knew.

He unzipped the tent and stuck his head in.

"Are you coming back out?" he said. I nodded. He held out his hand.

ANOTHER CARLOAD OF people arrived, with shrieks and laughter— they'd gotten lost, claiming Vermont exits all looked identical. It was Alex and Sophie and Nina, who'd graduated before us, and a few people I didn't recognize. There was a guy with long curly hair and a beard, a UMASS T-shirt, and a hemp necklace. He was hugging everyone, including the people he was meeting for the first time.

"Noel?" I said.

He looked up.

"Zuzu." He gave me a small wave before he and Sophie set up

their tent. For a while I watched the muscles in his back, underneath his T-shirt. He had never been so cool toward me; he usually approached with his arms flung out, seeking an embrace I never wanted to give.

He knew, I thought. Nobody else glanced at Cash or at me. Our absence had been unremarkable, people wandered off all the time, and we were good friends. Perhaps Noel could see the slight change in my skin, the flush of being recently overwhelmed. It was the only time I could think of when it seemed like he didn't want to touch me.

All I wanted was for Cash to come to bed with me, but the night was endless, more music, more beer. We were sitting on opposite sides of the campfire, and once he looked at me and winked, which was very un-Cash-like. I gave up around one thirty and went into the tent and crawled into my borrowed sleeping bag, and when I felt someone land beside me, I put a hand on the back that I thought belonged to Cash. I felt warm, soft skin and a tank top strap.

"Who is this?"

"Nina. Sorry." She laughed. "We decided to crash wherever because it's so late."

I didn't answer. I lay in the dark, listening to Nina breathe. Eventually Hugh came in alone. I could hear Noel laughing out there, then after a while only the snap of the fire. When I sat up, sweat ran down my back. Hugh or Nina let out a sleepy *shhh* when I unzipped the tent.

Outside, Molly was lying on a blanket, her feet kicked up behind her, her legs golden both in and out of the firelight. Cash was next to her on his back, gesturing with a stick as they talked. She rolled onto her back, then onto her stomach again, and said something that made Cash laugh. Wind tossed a handful of embers in their direction, and they fell to the blanket and burned tiny holes.

Reunion

Cash was already at a table in the hotel bar, sipping a drink. He had a tiny cut on his jaw.

"You shaved," I said.

"You're wearing a hat." He stood up and gave me a terrible hug. "I got you a gin and tonic."

"In February?"

"It's hot in here. Practically summer."

I sat down. There was a small saucer of wasabi peas, untouched, and another of salted nuts. I started to fill my mouth from both saucers, stinging my tongue.

"How's Gideon?"

"He's good. Up in the Adirondacks with a friend, actually. Drinking gallons of hot chocolate, from what I've been told. And how's Portia?"

"Good, good." He reached for his phone and showed me a photo. "Mud pies are kind of her thing right now."

"Cute."

"Listen, I'm sorry about your father."

"I know. I know." I held up my hands. "I just went through the whole memorial service. I need a break from that stuff right now, if you don't mind."

"Well. Okay. But it would be totally uncouth if I hadn't said something."

"Maybe you *are* totally uncouth."

He finished his drink, and another appeared on a tray, along with a dish of pickled vegetables he must have ordered before I arrived, and two small wax-paper bags of house-fried potato chips. The bar was famous for these, among other things. The cocktail napkins looked as if they were inlaid with gold. Everything felt heavy and ornate, sturdy and serious. Everything was a blanket I could crawl underneath with Cash.

I sipped the gin and tonic, even though it wasn't really what I wanted. Cash looked at the mural on the wall. I stared at my wedding ring, a princess-cut diamond set in a braided band. Sometimes it looked childish to me. I had never washed the ring, not once, in all the years I had worn it.

"Are we talking, or are we just sitting here," Cash said.

"We're talking." I sat back in my chair. "So I thought I ran into Molly in the lobby."

"Molly is nowhere near that lobby, trust me. They're up at her parents' place for the long weekend. We decided it was too much for Portia to be stuck in here." He took a wasabi pea, then dropped it back in the dish. "You never said why you're in Boston."

"Visiting Heidi."

"Who's Heidi?"

"Oh, just the woman my wife probably should have married."

"Nicer version of you, huh?"

I bit an ice cube from my drink.

"I'm nice."

"You're not," he said. "Not really."

"Neither are you."

"We're a good match, then." He took his swizzle stick and tapped the side of my glass.

"Should we get you something else? You don't seem that into this."

"I don't know," I said.

"We don't have to sit here if you don't want to," he said. "We can go somewhere else."

"Like where?"

"Room 318." He spun his key card on the table. "I have a present for you up there anyway."

He signed the check, tipping beyond the automatic 20 percent. His watch looked so heavy I wondered if you could throw it at a window and break the glass.

"Shall we?" he said.

I adjusted my hat as we left the bar and walked through the lobby. When I pressed the button to call the elevator, Cash touched my shoulder.

"Actually, I'm going to take the stairs," he said.

"What? Why?"

"I'll meet you up there. Room 318," he said.

I STOOD ALONE in the mirrored box as it rose. The low light was flattering, but I was starting to hate my hat, and to regret, deeply, that all my hair products sat in a zippered pouch in Heidi's cottage.

The elevator stopped at the second floor to admit a couple holding tennis rackets, presumably having played at the club adjacent to the hotel. I had a private ritual with people like this, where I placed in their view whatever was most expensive about me, to assure them that I belonged, that I knew where I was, that I had quite possibly gone to law school with them or their friends. I leaned back and crossed my ankles, sure that the woman would notice my boots, which she did. I felt her approval, a quick, warm current, and ignored the cool lick of her curiosity.

CASH ANSWERED MY knock. His watch was off, his sleeves rolled up, and he was barefoot. He looked as if he'd been there for an hour. The television was on, and he was drinking from a large bottle of mineral water. The opulence of the bar and lobby had been abandoned in the rooms, which had been redone to achieve the kind of monochromatic minimalism our generation liked. The linens were ivory, the cushioned headboard charcoal gray, and the whole bed was on a slight platform. The walls were papered in tawny grass cloth and a fire burned behind glass in the gas fireplace.

"How were the stairs?" I said.

"Good. I needed to move my legs a little." He stood back to let me in. "How was the elevator?"

"Unremarkable." I sat on the cushioned bench at the end of the bed to untie my boots.

He fell backward onto the bed, dislodging some of the decorative pillows. I pulled off one boot, then the other, then wasn't sure where to sit. I looked at Cash, who was lounging in apparent comfort, watching the local weather report.

"Are we talking, or just sitting here," I said.

He looked at the ceiling.

"Cash," I said.

"I don't know." He set the bottle of mineral water on one of the nightstands and drummed his stomach. "Tell me a story, Zuzu."

It was too awkward to stay on the bench; it felt like I was approaching a dignitary. It seemed too suggestive to lie beside him, so I sat as far away from him on the bed as possible, with better than usual posture. I set my hat between us. I kept my hands on my knees. The fact that I was due to have dinner at my mother's later that night—with Agnes, no less—felt comically improbable, a plan for a different person with a different life.

"What kind of story," I said.

"A good one."

"I don't have any good ones."

"Tell me a funny one, then. Tell me a funny story about us in college."

"I don't know. We were idiots."

"Maybe on occasion."

"I spent a lot of time back then worrying you were going to sleep with Molly Pierce."

"Ah."

"Turns out you married Molly Pierce."

"That I did." He started to drum his stomach again, then stopped. He smoothed the duvet with his hand, and left his hand next to my arm. "My wife is mad at me all the time, Zuzu. I mean *all* the time."

"So is mine."

"No, I mean, she's right. Molly deserves a lot more than I have delivered, of late." He ran a finger from the center of my wrist to my inner elbow. "And what have you done to poor Agnes?"

"None of your business."

"You're right. Totally."

"Shut up," I said. "I wasn't serious."

He withdrew his hand.

"Our house would fall apart if it weren't for Molly," he said. "There'd be like two pieces of celery in the fridge and no milk. None of the bills would get paid. Portia's hair would be in a giant knot. The cars would be unregistered. We'd never go on vacation. It would all go down in flames, honestly. And on top of managing family stuff, she has clients."

"So you're totally incompetent, and she lets you get away with it."

"Not anymore." He shook his head against the pillow. "She's had it."

"Well, what does she want?"

"Gratitude. Acknowledgment. I like, never thank her, which is pretty fucked up."

I tried to imagine Agnes, lying in bed with Heidi, wishing she'd thanked me more.

I began to laugh.

"What's funny?"

"My wife does *not* wish she thanked me more. At this point I'm mostly a nuisance."

"Zuzu." He shifted away and took a sip of water. "Come on. Don't say that."

"I don't mean all the time, but . . . Look. Look at this." I unlocked my phone and started scrolling through old photos.

"You have *proof*?"

"Just read it."

ZUZU: ugh flat tire fuckkkkk

AGNES: oh no! call the roadside people

ZUZU: I did they said 2-3 hours

AGNES: hope you brought a book;)

ZUZU: I thought u were working from home today

AGNES: I'm on calls until well after 19:00

ZUZU: I am literally 15 min from the house

ZUZU: lmk if you have a break . . . maybe u could
change it for me so the day isn't wasted

AGNES: you are a smart, capable woman, you can
figure this out

ZUZU: figure out how to change a tire right now? R
u serious?

AGNES: yes

Cash handed the phone back to me and whistled.

"I don't know what you want me to say."

"I probably shouldn't have shown it to you in the first place."

"Probably not." He scratched his chest. "So what happened?"

"She came and changed it. She wasn't going to leave me stranded. She just gets so annoyed with me."

"Have you learned how to change a tire since then?"

"Yeah, right. How about you do it."

"If I am ever called upon to change a tire for you, I will do it. No problem." His hand came down over mine. "Should we watch a movie?"

"No. We should not watch a movie," I said. He stared at the TV. I watched him breathe. Our quiet indecision filled me with bitter doubt. I did not think a truly beautiful woman would have to wait like this or hope like this. He turned and rolled his body onto mine, his face in my throat, his arms limp on either side of my body. He wanted only to be held. I held him, one hand on the back of his neck. Two minutes passed. I wanted to turn off the fire, but not enough to move him.

"And then they lay on a bed in silence until she got up and left," Cash said.

"So you want me to go?"

"I was describing the scene."

"Ah." I looked down at his hair. It had lost none of its thickness. On the TV, an ad for a local car dealership in central Mass came on, its jingle unchanged since I was a child. "The scene sounds bad," I said.

"It's not great." He rolled off me, stretched his arms over his head. "Not great, but not a surprise."

"Meaning?"

"Meaning you are *the* most passive person I've met in my life."

"I am not." I sat up and took a sip of his water. "You know, I left Agnes at Heidi's house at two in the morning. That's not exactly passive." I untied my sweater and pulled it off, snapping the straps of the silk camisole. "Also, I bought this today."

"Nice," he said. He barely looked at the tops of my breasts. I hated him, mostly for whatever quality made my hatred of him so thin and transient. I still wanted, I still wanted.

I thought the scale of my wanting would repulse him. I feared if I opened my mouth he would feel me trying to swallow him whole.

"I guess I shouldn't have asked you up here," he said.

"Whatever, it's fine."

"I have a wife. *You* have a wife. There are two wives to consider here."

"There are three," I said. "If I count for anything."

"I—sorry. You know what I mean." He rested his fingers on my wrist for four, five seconds. This emboldened me.

"Why did you take the stairs and leave me alone in the elevator?"

"Because you're almost forty, and I figured you could take an elevator by yourself."

Invoking forty, I thought, had just enough teasing in it to let me try to punch him, which I did. He grabbed my arm and twisted it, giving me an excuse to collapse against him, which I did. He lay on his back and I pressed my face to his chest. I thought of how, if she wanted to, Molly could lie like this every day.

"Can I ask you something?" I said. "Are you and Molly okay?"

"No," he said. "I don't know. No."

I sat up.

"What am I doing here in this tacky hotel with you?"

"Tacky?"

"Why am I even here, Cash?"

"You said you would be in town, and I asked you to have a drink. Pretty standard stuff. I get an email like that from somebody once a month."

"And do you always lie on top of the person you're drinking with at these monthly events?"

He rolled away from me and rose from the bed, brushing off his pants as if they were covered in crumbs.

"I forgot about your gift," he said.

"What gift."

He crossed the room, reached behind an overstuffed chair, pulled out a paper bag, and shook its contents onto the floor. A dark pile of fabric fell out, and a gold-wrapped box fell on top of that. He tossed the box to me and I caught it.

"What is this?" I said, lifting the lid.

The marzipan was shaped like fruit and arranged in rainbow order on a bed of gold-flecked paper. Marzipan strawberries, followed by marzipan mandarin oranges with tender green leaves that broke under the pressure of my thumb. Lifting a mandarin, I almost flattened it between my fingers before I placed it on my tongue. My eyes felt hot, my tongue heavy with sugary paste.

"Don't cry," he said.

I swallowed the mandarin.

"Thank you."

"Yeah, of course."

"It's so good."

"I tried one at the store."

"I can't believe you actually got me condolence marzipan." I put the lid back on the box, restored by the almond, and by the fact that Cash paid so much attention to the things I said.

"Oh, and don't forget this," he said, throwing the second item at me, which I recognized, once it fell across my lap, as the Vineyard sweatshirt I'd believed to be in my storage unit.

"No," I said.

"You left it when you came to visit me when I lived in Somerville."

I held it up by its sleeves. The navy color had faded considerably.
The *V* was almost gone.

"No," I said. "I thought this was . . . I thought I had this somewhere else." I tugged the sweatshirt over my silk camisole. "You
know this was my father's, right?"

He shook his head no.

"Well, it was. His. My father's."

"I'm so sorry."

"I thought this was rotting in a storage unit."

"Nope. Just in my closet."

"I mean, for *years* I've been thinking I had to drive there and dig
through our stuff to find it."

"I'm glad I remembered to bring it this time."

"Don't congratulate yourself! I have been looking for this for
God knows how long, and you were holding on to it until you felt
like giving it back."

"I guess I kept forgetting. I'm sorry."

"You've moved like fifteen times since you lived in Somerville.
You packed this up fifteen times, and it never occurred to you to
give it back?"

"It *did* occur to me," he said. "The whole reason I didn't throw it
away years ago is that I knew you'd want it."

I was dizzy, as if I'd taken shots on an empty stomach. Shots on an empty stomach had been part of my life with Cash, who had held on to a piece of my clothing for over a decade, not by accident, but because he cared about it, because he wanted something that was mine.

"Here's an idea," I said. "You could just say that you liked having it."

"Honestly, I didn't think about it."

"Bullshit. You carried it around with you. You packed it every time you moved."

"Yeah, I mean, it was in my closet."

"Because you *wanted* it there!"

He turned and went into the bathroom and closed the door, and before I followed him I took off the sweatshirt and buried my face in the word "Vineyard." I willed myself to summon the history of that cotton, pleaded with my feet to feel, instead of thick hotel carpet, cool grains of packed wet sand. I wanted stinging bites on my arms and legs, as if I were on a beach at dusk. I wanted to have no idea where my shoes were, I wanted not to care. I wanted to taste Atlantic salt. Like my father, I loved the beach at low tide the most. I believed in it sincerely, in the promise it seemed to be making, which was that I could walk without limit, that I could actually brush up against what I saw, burn my hands on the sunset and keep walking.

I opened the bathroom door without knocking. It startled Cash, though he was just standing by the towel rack. He walked away from me, as if the marble floor were a long corridor. The corridor ended at a deep soaking tub, and he climbed inside it.

"You should take a bath with me," he said, sliding all the way down, his feet up on the marble ledge. "Maybe it'll calm you down."

I dropped the sweatshirt on the floor. He smiled at me as I approached, laughing and moving to the far corner of the tub when I leaned over and turned on the water. His clothes were getting soaked, but he sat there, shaking his head in the rising steam.

"You're insane," he said.

In fact, I did feel that I'd lost control of my ability to make measured decisions. I rolled my pants up and sat on the edge of the tub, dipping my toes in.

"Christ, it's hot," I said.

He sat there, his clothes blooming underwater. My feet drifted by his. He did not touch me.

"This is stupid," I said.

"It's not how I saw the day going."

"You didn't think I'd follow you in here."

"No." He shifted in his shallow pool. "This is a little crazy, Zuzu."

"You said, quote, 'You should take a bath with me.'"

Both of us watched the steaming water pour from the faucet. I lifted my feet out of the tub.

"What you want me to say, and what I actually feel?" He held his hands shoulder-width apart. "Those are two different things. I'm sorry to tell you, but they are."

"You don't want me, is what you're saying."

"Not—no, that's not what I said."

"So say it. Like say it plainly. Just say it."

"You want me to say it."

"I just said to say it."

"I don't understand you," he said. I stood up, slipping as I crossed the room.

"Careful you don't fall," Cash said.

I picked the sweatshirt up off the floor and shook it. "I don't want this anymore, by the way. I don't, you don't, my father can't. Nobody does."

He leaned forward to open the drain.

"Just take it," he said. "You might want it later."

I picked up the gilt-edged sewing kit, compliments of the hotel, next to an apothecary jar full of cotton balls. Agnes loved hotel sewing kits, and even though I did not—I always found them months later, shoved in a drawer, untouched—I took it for her, as if a small, free gift for my wife were a great slight to him.

"I'm sorry, Zuzu," Cash said, which I found to be even less tolerable than *careful you don't fall*.

I took the sweatshirt with me when I left, and then I was back in the elevator where I'd so recently tilted my ankles to show off my expensive boots in the warm pour of recessed light. In the bright, polished lobby, I left my father's sweatshirt on an upholstered bench.

Why Isn't She Thinking About Her Father More Often

M aybe I had ceded that ground to Julia. She was the one who loved him more; she was the daughter who got to mourn.

But I must have been thinking about him, because when one of his favorite songs came on the car radio, I hit the power button so fast and so hard it left a red mark on my hand.

Trespassers

June 1, 2008

The wedding invitation surprised me—it was from Alex, who'd lived in the vegetarian house, and Sophie, his pregnant girlfriend. When I complained to Agnes about attending without a date, she said she'd be happy to join me. "It will be fun to see you at your precious alma mater," she said, which made me consider how much I still talked about school, four years after I'd left.

I RENTED A Zipcar, insisting that the drive would be beautiful, and it was, the Taconic damp and green. We stopped for biscuits and gravy at the twenty-four-hour diner near campus, wearing paper napkins tucked into the necklines of our dresses. "These taste like they came from a mix," Agnes said of the biscuits.

"You know they're delicious," I said.

"I can make better biscuits than these."

I threw a crumpled napkin at her, and it landed in her cup of coffee.

"Oops."

"You did me a favor," she said, laughing.

I texted Cash, who had been noncommittal about his attendance: James A. Cashel III, are you coming?

Yeah, stuck in traffic, he wrote.

The ceremony was brief, in a sweltering tent set up before the famous library. Noel Rafferty sat several rows behind me, wearing seersucker and mouthing something to me that I couldn't catch; later, he told me he'd just been saying hello. Whenever I glanced at him he was drinking champagne and laughing too loudly, trying to compensate, I thought, for the fact that everyone else there had graduated. It was how I sometimes felt, years later, among Agnes and her colleagues, when I was the only one in the room who hadn't been able to pass the bar.

MOLLY'S DRESS WAS raw silk with an asymmetrical hemline, and her necklace was so big that Agnes later described it as a breastplate. Molly was in graduate school—she wanted to be a therapist—and she looked like an actual adult. She had undergone what I thought of as that year's sudden transformation, as if we all knew what was coming—how in a matter of weeks we were going to be talking, nonstop, about Lehman Brothers; how at the law school we were going to wonder if there would still be jobs for us by the time we graduated. There was plenty of talk about how bankruptcy law was now "hot," and for a time I would answer questions about my future practice area by saying "bankruptcy, most likely," which always satisfied whoever had asked.

We were starting to buy furniture, instead of draping fabric over folding chairs (more than one of my friends had done this to make a "couch.") We were attending weddings by ourselves. Molly and I had an exchange about showing up without dates, and Agnes had interrupted to say, "Technically, I'm your date." I said, rather too quickly, "Yep, I'm here with a friend," as if to tamp down any suspicion, but later the suspicions turned out to be mine. Approaching Agnes with her third drink in my hand, I admired, from a distance, the subtle gestures she made when she talked, slight turns of her wrist that were still growing familiar to me; she was, my mother once remarked, a born salesperson, not through charisma but through conviction. Agnes always believed what she said. She took the drink from me without looking in my direction, and this made me feel that we had the kind of connection I often noticed in other couples. I felt a quickening, not in my chest but in the speed of the sweat dripping down my neck, when I caught, in my private thoughts, that phrase: "other couples." Her dress exposed much of her back, and the heat had turned her skin pink against the pattern of goldenrod.

CASH WAS STUCK in traffic for so long that he missed the ceremony. Too bad, he wrote. I'm almost there.

A few minutes later, another text: @ vegetarian house. Empty &
unlocked. Meet me on the roof?

I wrote, Aren't you trespassing?

Not trespassing. This is our house.

You're trespassing, darling, I wrote.

THE RECEPTION WAS at a banquet hall, and there was a shuttle
from the nearby hotel, but I said I wanted to get my money's worth
from the Zipcar. The truth was that I didn't feel ready to leave campus yet. I asked Agnes if she wanted to see the library. I thought she
would like to take her time, to behold the beauty of the stonework.
I told her to tip her head back and look at the way the sun came
through the highest windows, how it happened to strike a collection
of blue-bound journals and a cluster of green armchairs. At a certain
time of day, I told her, it was like reading underwater.

"I think it's sweet, how much it means to you," she said.

WAITING PATIENTLY, CASH texted while I showed Agnes the library. When we were walking back to the car, I received a second
text: waiting less patiently now.

"My dumb friend wants me to swing by our old house for a
second," I said. "Do you mind?"

"Me?" She shook her head. "I'm just along for the ride today,
aren't I?"

"I couldn't have dealt with all of this without you," I said.

"Why not?" she said. "These people are your friends."

I BELIEVED, AT that time, that Cash was waiting for me alone. I believed that the roof was a place where he might want to make a confession or a declaration; barring that, I believed that he and I shared an agreement that our spot on the roof was sacred and reserved for us. When Agnes and I pulled up, the first thing I noticed was the light on Molly's breastplate necklace, and the seersucker jacket—Noel's—she held loosely around her shoulders. There were three or four others up there, but I stopped looking and turned to Agnes, who was nibbling crackers she'd brought in the car. She had a fresh burn on her arm that I knew to be from bacon grease; it had happened when she'd asked me over for brunch the previous weekend. My only job had been to make the mimosas, and I'd spilled the orange juice everywhere.

"What?" she said.

"You're very pretty."

"Shut up. Are you good to drive?"

"I'm serious," I said.

She offered me a cracker and I shook my head.

"Are you going up, or what?"

"I don't think so," I said. "I mean, aren't they trespassing?"

"Probably? I don't know."

"I don't need to sit on a roof today. Not in this dress."

"Your call," she said.

"No roof," I said, pulling away from the curb. We crossed the Mid-Hudson Bridge and went as far as New Paltz before I admitted that I didn't feel like going to the reception.

"Would it be horrible?" I said. "Would it be unforgivable?"

"I don't know," she said. "Aren't they going to miss you?"

"They'll survive."

"Yay," she said. "I'm happy to have you all to myself. But if we're this dressed up, where should we go?"

"Martinis."

"Where's that?"

"No," I said, laughing. "We should be holding martini glasses. Look at us. Our nails are painted."

We drove to a small hotel Mom and Glenn had once stayed in when they came to visit me at school, and we drank martinis alone in the dark bar, reserved a room with two beds, bemoaned our lack of comfortable clothes, split an order of steak frites, went out to the small pool and hot tub and rolled our dresses up and dangled our feet in the bubbling water. We talked about our senior proms: I had gone with a guy friend who ended the night by asking me if I thought men could ever "really" be bisexual. She went with someone who threw up on the dance floor. She called her parents, who picked up both her and her drunk date, dropped him off at home, then asked her if she wanted to return to the dance. Agnes told me that she had said yes because she thought it was the right answer.

The Cashels

November 2040

There is no question that I would have changed my name to his. Years of dismissing the practice as archaic and possessive would have dissolved instantly if I could have been folded into the Cashels.

What strikes me about my daydream house—beyond its lack of originality and its reliance on furniture catalogues—is its disorder: The imaginary rooms are overrun with evidence of a busy life. A deep farmhouse sink with dishes inside it. Marble countertops stacked with plates, scattered with cocktail napkins. On the plates: olive pits, cracker crumbs. A pitcher with a red crust of sugar on the glass, discs of orange stuck to the sides: What is this? Sangria, which I love and which Cash made for me our sophomore year, mixing it in a thick plastic box that he'd emptied of pencils and binder clips. *What?* he'd said. *It's an all-purpose container.*

That version of the Cashels—the Susan and James version—would have added a sangria set to their registry. That version of me wouldn't have balked at the idea of a registry, the way Agnes and I did—"It's too tacky!"—so that each time we spent two hundred dollars on a friend's wedding gift, I felt they owed us something in return.

IN THE HOUSE I imagined sharing with Cash, in our sixties we threw the kinds of parties where people wound up sleeping on the couch. Roaming the daydream rooms, I saw gray-haired Molly Pierce under my husband's Glacier National Park blanket, and I was glad to have her there, because the party was mine and I could afford to be generous. I would have been a person who flung her doors open, who liked the place full, who didn't mind dishes and crumbs, who was too content, too warm and sticky with sangria, too assured of my place next to him in our bed to worry about crooked bath mats, water rings on wooden tables, clutter on windowsills, shoes kicked off and left in the hall, records (if you marry Cash, you have vinyl records) out of their sleeves. I could have been, in that life, a dog person, the type who didn't mind taking out a bowl and whisking eggs and seeing, as she whisks, a strand of dog hair. The type who sees that and says *oh, well* instead of frantically scouring the bowl. The type who isn't worried about a little mess, who feels loved, who feels sufficiently desired, who thinks the mess is just part of the splendor.

The Favor

⌒

I had to be wanted, unequivocally, for a moment. I had to.

I knocked on his door.

"It's me," I said as he opened it.

"Julia and Perry are at their baby class at the hospital." He was in the same flannel shirt and jeans he'd been wearing when he picked me up from the train, but he'd added an unzipped fleece and a watchman's cap. "Come on in. I'm working on my grocery list."

"Fun!"

"Not really." He pushed the bowl on his table toward me. "Take a grape."

I sat down and took a grape, chewing it slowly, taking stock of what else was scattered across the table: some kind of tech manual, a highlighter, a tube of breath mints with liquid centers, and an L.L.Bean catalogue. The vacuum was in the middle of the small living area, its cord running wild. Over his shoulder I could see that his bed had been stripped.

"Need something, Zuzu?" He tore a page out of his notebook.

"You eat a lot of fruit," I said.

He was still folding the paper in his hands.

"Excuse me?"

"The last time I was here, there were a lot more grapes."

He tucked the folded paper into his pocket.

"Never mind," I said. "I'm having a kind of personal emergency."

"There's an urgent care—"

"Not that kind of emergency. Just need to sit still for a minute, I think."

He flipped open a metal tin on the table and withdrew his keys. Something about him had changed. I wondered if he felt more confident with the hat. My own hat felt a bit like a shield, and I touched its brim. "Anyway, I was on my way out to the store," he said. "You're welcome to use the shower if you need it, or I can let you into Julia's."

"Do I look that dirty?"

"No."

"Yeah I do. You must be wondering why I keep showing up here unbathed."

He clasped his hands behind his back and stretched.

"All right," he said. "Take your time, I'll be out for a while."

"I'm not going to use your shower, Noel."

"That's your call." He thumped the wall, right above his calendar, and closed the door behind him.

I took off my hat and rested my head on my arms for a bit. I ate four more grapes.

On my phone: nothing from Cash, nothing from Agnes.

In Noel's freezer: rainbow sherbet, which struck me as both endearing and embarrassing.

His bedroom smelled like glass cleaner. His mattress had a quilted top with a pattern of blue flowers, a divorced man's brandnew bed.

I glanced in his closet, behind the bathroom mirror, under the sink: There was no evidence of the ex-wife anywhere. To avoid falling and breaking a bone, I coiled the vacuum cord back into place. Under his couch, I found a pair of ten-pound weights. Like his bare mattress and the sherbet, this embarrassed me; I thought maybe the weights should have been heavier. I checked my phone for messages from Agnes or Cash: still nothing. I sat at Noel's small table and pulled the notebook out from under the fruit bowl. I remembered that he had sometimes sketched people back in school; I remembered that people had said it was "gay" to draw your classmates for no reason, also that it was "gay" that his sketch pad had a purple cover. I remembered that he had won an award for a self-portrait his senior year.

Maybe there are drawings of me in here, is an actual thought I had.

He kept his grocery lists and crossed them out. I flipped past a few and saw the same items over and over. He liked tomato soup and crackers, blueberry yogurt, frozen peas, whole wheat bread. It looked not unlike the list I might have written if I had been single at our age. Of course, I knew nothing of what it would be like to shop just for myself at any point in my thirties.

I heard his keys jangling. I pushed his open notebook to my right.

"You didn't shower yet?" He pushed a case of tonic water into the room with his foot.

"What's that for? Are you having a party?"

He turned for the rest of his bags. There was something familiar in the way he lifted the bags to the counter, opened the fridge, put the milk in the door. Silence, no eye contact, the *thunk* of someone completing their tasks: This was Agnes.

"Noel? Hello? Can you hear me?"

He broke the seal on a bottle of hand soap and set it next to his sink.

"Sorry. My ex-wife just announced she's stopping by later today to get something, and I'm not especially looking forward to that." He handed me a bag of oranges, and I ripped the netting open and let them fall in among the grapes. He went back to the counter, picked up a jar of instant coffee, and shook it at me. "I'm going to have some. Am I correct that you're too fancy for this?"

"Yes," I said. "I'm too fancy."

I checked my email while he made instant coffee. Nothing from Agnes, nothing from Cash. I thanked Theresa for a raft of photos she'd sent of Gideon and Reid, playing with sticks in front of Mirror Lake, far from the mess I was making across the state of Massachusetts. Then I turned my phone off and slid it into my pocket. Something was different about Noel, and it wasn't just the watchman's cap. He slurped his instant coffee and looked at me.

"What," I said.

"What were you looking for, anyway? Did you think that was my secret diary?"

"I don't know." I flipped a page in his notebook. "I wanted to see if you buy the same thing every week."

"More or less, yeah."

"You love routines."

"I do." He nodded. "I find them helpful."

His phone had started ringing while he made his coffee. We sat through a second round of ringing, then a third.

"Is there an emergency or something?" I said.

He glanced down at the screen.

"My ex-wife feels like talking," he said. "Guess what? I don't." He got up from the table. "You hungry? You want something before you go?"

"No."

"You want some toast?"

"No, thank you."

"Well, I'm hungry."

"I'll make you something." I stood up. "I have too much energy to just sit here, anyway. What do you want? A sandwich?"

"Zuzu. You're not making me a *sandwich*."

"Maybe I am making you a sandwich." I reached around him and grabbed the bread off the counter. "Maybe you can't stop me."

He took the bread away from me. I took it back, raised it above my head, and threw it across the room. His look of shock and confusion was delightful to me.

"I can't believe you just did that," he said.

"I know. Poor organic whole grain."

He pulled me forward by the front of my jeans, his knuckles on my skin.

"Noel," I said.

He dropped his hand. "You don't think I'll do it."

"Do what."

He scratched the back of his neck, a nervous gesture of his I had forgotten about. He had recited "After Apple-Picking" in English our junior year of high school, and our teacher had made him recite it twice, *The second time without clawing at your nape, please.* I'd chosen a Rita Dove poem, holding my hands behind my back to avoid admonitions about my nape.

"I've had enough rejection from you," he said. "I'm quite familiar with it."

"I can't reject you," I said, "unless you're making some kind of advance."

"I'm not making an advance."

I looked at my fingernails.

"Okay," I said. "I'll leave, then."

"You'll stay if I tell you how pretty you are."

"I didn't hear anything about how pretty I am."

"You already know," he said. "So there's no need to tell you."

He picked up his cup of instant coffee and turned to set it in the sink. I studied the width of his shoulders.

"Zuzu."

"What."

"You want to come with me to run an errand for your sister? Somebody in town is giving a baby swing away for free." He picked up his keys and tossed them back and forth between his hands. "Perry was supposed to get it, actually, but he ran out of time so I said I'd do it."

"Okay," I said.

THE BEST ROUTE to the house with the baby swing was to cut through the state park. Above us, maple trees conferred, tipping their winter-stripped heads, and I imagined the deep green shadow they would have granted us by late May.

The house was long, low, and white, and its six gabled windows had diamond panes. I remembered opening one of those windows and exhaling a mouthful of smoke into the cold night air.

"This is Val Miller's house," I said. "At least it was in 1998."

"Val Miller was a bitch."

"Oh, my God. You can't say bitch anymore."

"Pretend it's 1998." He smiled. "No name on the mailbox. Also, interestingly, no baby swing in the driveway, as promised."

"You could go knock," I said.

"You could go knock."

"No way."

"She was *your* friend, not mine."

"No." I shook my head. "She was pretty mean. But her parents were never home and they had a real bar in there. Bitters, cherries, vermouth. Everything."

"I wouldn't know," he said. "I was never invited."

"You didn't miss much."

I looked at the house. I had no linear memory, but plenty of bursts: blowing smoke out the diamond-paned window. Black-light posters, menthols, Fiona Apple, red wine and Sprite. Nirvana, Garbage, Hole. A shower with a frosted door, using Val Miller's razor to shave my legs, getting ready for a dance where nothing was going to happen.

"Can we agree that there's no swing here?" Noel said.

"Confirmed. There is no swing here."

He started to drive.

"I liked Val's boyfriend," I said. "One time he told me I looked really good with my hair wet. So guess what I did."

"I can't imagine."

"I carried a spray bottle around," I said.

"You did not."

"I did." I hadn't thought of it in years. "I carried a spray bottle in my backpack, and it leaked on all my stuff. Every fifteen minutes I tried to get my hair wet all over again so I would look good."

He whistled.

"I hated *air*, Noel. I hated the radiators at school. They were ruining my look."

He slowed the car down and pulled to the side of the road. We were inside the park. It looked gray and freezing in every direction. He unbuckled his seat belt and turned to face me.

"Just think, all that time, you could've been hanging out with me," he said.

I laughed and wiped my nose.

"I was busy."

"Doing what? Making collages? Taping music off the radio? Sneaking a cigarette on the roof, or whatever, with your mean friends?"

I felt tightness in my chest, exacerbated by the seat belt, which I unbuckled and pushed aside. I twisted in the seat to face him.

"All of the above," I said. Not a single car had passed us. There wasn't enough snow for cross-country skiing, and the ice on the small pond was too thin and weak to bear weight. I wanted to exude something other than anger. I wanted to stay beautiful to at least one person. Idling outside of Val Miller's house for two minutes had pushed me briefly back into that era, which was to say that I felt both weepy and unclear about what would happen next.

"It's okay if you don't," I said, "but do you still like me?"

I thought he might laugh. I sounded, to my own ears, like I was whispering to him in an empty classroom, that we were in our blazers and we were about to be late for lunch. We had lived, for a time, in a world of chalkboard dust and radiator heat. We had worried about getting a B+. Noel grabbed my hands and brought them both to his face, pressing my palms to his cheeks. He kissed my knuckles. "I'm not going to do anything, I promise," he said, kissing my knuckles again, and I said that I wouldn't either.

New Swing

Julia was waiting for us on her front steps. She wore a knit purple-and-green argyle dress, the diamonds expanded over her belly. Her curls looked slightly crisp, as if she'd used the wrong setting on her hair dryer.

"The swing wasn't there," I said, rolling down the window as I spoke. "Somebody else must have taken it. So we wound up running to the store to buy you one instead."

"You shouldn't have done that," she said. "How much was it?"

"Don't worry about it."

"People are looking for you two," she said. "Agnes called me because she was starting to worry—she said you haven't been answering your phone?"

"Oh. Sound must be turned off."

"And you," she said, looking at Noel, "have a guest waiting upstairs."

"She's here?" He was already opening his door. "How long has she been here?"

"I don't know, Noel. Ten minutes?"

He looked at me. "I have to go."

I waved him away and opened his trunk, struggling with the baby swing. It had been his idea to buy one, to explain why we took so long.

"What'd you do to him, Zuzu?" Julia said. "He looked so nervous."

"Maybe he's nervous because his ex-wife is up there waiting to kill him."

"Maybe. I don't really know her." Julia shrugged. "Anyway, I'm going to tag along with you to have dinner at Mom's. That okay?"

She told me to leave the box by the front door—"Let Perry deal with it later"—and when we got into my car, I braced myself for the moment she would figure out what had happened between me and Noel. She was scrolling on her phone.

"I'm hot," I said. "I'm going to crack the windows."

"Fine with me. I'm always hot right now."

"Be warned," I said, backing out of her driveway. "Last time Mom served plain spaghetti—she forgot she didn't have any sauce—and a bowl of iceberg lettuce with oil and vinegar."

"Ugh."

"That was one of her better dinners."

"Ha," Julia said.

I turned onto the road, keeping her close to the subject of Trish, which would push us further from the subject of Noel.

What'd you do to him, Zuzu? had perhaps not been the right question. The better question, I thought, was to ask what he had done to me. I understood that his promise—*I'm not going to do anything*—was something he felt he had to say, and in fact continued to say while we performed the awkward task of unbuttoning and unzipping in a confined space.

Above him, I wasn't sure what to do. I held his face. I kissed his head.

"Are you always this weird with men?" he said.

"Weird how?"

"Shaky? Uncomfortable?"

"I don't know," I said. "I don't remember."

I remembered that once, when Ethan asked if he was hurting me, I said no because I didn't think pain could be avoided, and I just wanted to get through it. I remembered how Cash's silence had unnerved me.

Noel let his fingers skate around. The touch was light, and I liked how it almost wasn't happening. You really do want me, I said. I really do, he said. Always have. His thumb came to my chin, then up to my mouth, and he pressed on my lip and I bit him.

The Castle

~

Our mother was at her stove, dipping a ladle in and out of a pot of soup, when Julia and I walked in.

"Shoes off, please."

"Oh, yes," I said. "The sacred rugs."

"They've been in Glenn's family for—"

"We know about the rugs, Mom," Julia said, prying off her boots.

It was still a bit unsettling to see Julia in that house, if only because there was nothing in there that belonged to her. My Doc Martens were still in the closet of my old third-floor bedroom, along with the purple cotillion dress Trish had urged me not to wear because it made me look "chesty." My friends had carved their initials into the back wall of that closet at my urging—not because I particularly loved them, but because of the social power they'd given me. I'd wanted proof.

"Julia," Trish said, kissing her cheek, "I broke up the bay leaf, and now I can't find the pieces."

I whistled.

"This kitchen has bay leaves?"

"What do you think?" Trish was looking only at my sister. "If any of us swallows a tiny bit of bay leaf, will that be all right?"

"What are you making?" I said.

She handed Julia the ladle. "See if you can get any more of it out?"

"Hello-o-o," I said.

"It's minestrone, Susan."

"You made minestrone from scratch?"

"You don't give me any credit. I didn't have *time* to cook when you two were young. Now I do."

Julia, basking in our mother's full attention, was trying to pick up a fleck of bay leaf with her fingers.

"I have to shower," I said. Neither of them looked up.

I BROUGHT IMAGINARY Noel to the shower with me, to go over what we'd done. I planted my hands on his imaginary wet chest. The real Noel had made a sound akin to crying, he had tried pulling at my hair, but I'd had it back in a knot to accommodate the hat. His lips on the backs of my fingers had been dry. It had been so abrupt, and so short. I opened my eyes under the beat of the water. I wondered if that was the last time I would ever sleep with a man.

DRESSED IN WHAT I could find in the closet—flannel pants and an unflattering, oversize white T-shirt—I brought my dirty clothes down to the laundry room. My mother was there, folding Glenn's socks and underwear. Glenn himself was on a golf outing with his brother in Arizona, which was one of the reasons my mother had originally suggested that Agnes and I spend the night. Trish didn't like to be in her large house all alone.

"Did you know Agnes is looking for you? She called to see if you were here yet."

"Okay," I said. "I'll call her back."

"She said you didn't answer your phone at all today."

"Battery."

She patted her tidy pile of clothes. "First time Agnes has called me looking for you in fifteen years."

"Uh-huh."

"She said you took off in the middle of the night and left her somewhere on the North Shore?"

"Does that sound like something I would do?"

She leaned forward with her elbows on the counter. She had lost just enough weight after marrying Glenn to fit into expensive yoga pants. Hers were black with purple stripes up the side, and she wore them with a fuzzy purple sweater. Her hair fell forward—naturally thick, with aggressive blond highlights, gray around the ears and at the roots. Her posture recalled, for me, the afternoon I'd come to tell her I was going to marry Agnes. We sat on the screened-in porch, in pine-green rocking chairs of which she and Glenn were amusingly proud; they'd won them in an auction, and they were supposedly quite valuable. I rocked, but my mother had kept her elbows locked right on her knees. Why so young, why so early, she wanted to know. Was one of us pregnant? She smirked when she said this. She had been pregnant with me when she married my father. Her parents, agonized at the thought of a mixed marriage, had offered her money to turn down his chip of a diamond ring. They relented. There was a church wedding, steak and chicken, cake and dancing. My mother deeply regretted her choice of dress—discounted, spangled, and heavily layered, picking up dust as she crossed the floor—and she used to let me and Julia play with it like any other toy.

"She's taking the train here tomorrow," Trish said, straightening up and shaking lint from an undershirt. "She gets into Springfield at ten thirty."

"I know."

"Can I say something here?"

"Of course."

"Okay. Well. Just listen. One of my regrets is the way Daddy and I still tried to have dinner together once we knew we were separating."

"Why would you bring that up?"

"It's just on my mind, that's all," she said.

"That was a great time for all of us. I loved watching him cry into his soup."

"Well, that's my point, Susan."

"And you pretended it wasn't happening."

"I hate to break it to you," she said, "but nobody gets to be proud of everything they've done. That's just not how it works."

"What is this, Trish's Wisdom?"

"Yeah, my wisdom," she said, dropping the folded clothes into a basket. She had always worn gloves to do housework, and her hands were in better condition than mine, less mottled and abraded from so many hours at the sink. Dishes could become the thing you thought about most in your life, if you let your life get that small. Dishes and piles of unopened mail and clothes left on the floor, you could drown in all of that. You could love your son to the point of worship and you could still find yourself gasping for air among the dirty plates.

THE MINESTRONE WAS too salty, and I let two scoops of oyster crackers disintegrate in it before I ate. Julia sat at the table, drinking a root beer and talking to Trish, who addressed me not a single time while she washed and dried the dishes. She went to bed promptly at nine, as she always did, and I asked Julia when she was going home.

"Unclear," she said, opening the pantry and staring at the shelves. "I'm still hungry. All I want to do is eat."

"She never has snacks."

"I know." She touched my elbow, and I thought she was going to ask me about Noel, or tell me how strange it had been to see us pull up in his car. Instead she said, "I need to lie down for a few minutes."

I followed her through the dining room, listening to the good plates tremble slightly in the built-in cabinets as we passed. At the far west side of the house was a room that Trish and Glenn more or less ignored, other than to keep it clean. It held Glenn's old keyboard ("Trish forbids me to use it within her hearing," he'd told me) and Julia's old waterbed, made up with a set of soft, mismatched sheets. There was an old, bulky TV on a stand, and a shelf of alphabetized DVDs. This was where Cash had slept, the time he came home with me for Thanksgiving.

"This is a time warp," I said, flopping onto the bed and feeling it undulate.

"Move over," Julia said. When she lay beside me it caused a surge beneath us. "Do you want to watch something?"

"Like what?"

"Pick a letter."

"Um." It amused me, how hot and meaningful certain letters felt: *C* and *N* and *A*. The first two were confessions, and the third should have been the answer. "*S*," I said.

She got out of the bed and knelt by the shelf of movies. She held up a case: *Splash*. One of our favorites when we were young.

"I'd like to be a mermaid," I said.

"Me too."

"I wish we had something sweet."

She looked over.

"Is there ice cream?"

"Doubt it. And I left like two pounds of marzipan at the hotel."

"What hotel?"

"Oh." I sat up. "Earlier today I went to see Cash, my friend from college? He gave me some marzipan but I left it there."

She was silent for several minutes, facing away from the movie.

"Are you asleep?" I said at last.

"No. But if I had been, that would've woken me up, dumbass." She rubbed her belly. "I was thinking about the one time I went to visit you at school your freshman year. You got so annoyed with me because you wanted to take me to this diner you loved but I really wanted to go to Olive Garden."

"I don't remember that."

"And then there was this film screening you were interested in, but Cash left a note on your door saying he might want to hang out later, so we pretty much sat in the common room all night waiting to see if he'd walk by."

"I have no recollection of this."

"Cash," she said. "Did I even meet him on that trip? I don't think I did."

"Hey." I patted her shoulder. "It's late. Are you sleeping over tonight?"

"No." She yawned. "I'll leave in a minute."

We fell asleep back-to-back, and I woke in the cool, once she was gone.

Questions for Noel

If when I kissed his chest he had noticed the gray in my hair, and if he still thought of me as beautiful, and if, given the chance, he would still make up reasons to get closer to me in the middle of the night, the way he had when he came downstairs for that glass of water?

The Fears

Outside the Springfield station my wife was holding a tray with two take-out coffees, and my first thought was that Heidi had come with her. Agnes wore a plaid skirt of several layers and a maroon coat with silver epaulets, neither of which I recognized. She loaded her bags into the trunk along with the duffel I'd left behind. As she settled into the passenger seat, I searched for signs of Heidi: a mark on the neck, a demonstrative scratch. Above her left ear Agnes wore a tiny barrette, possibly swiped from the side of Heidi's sink.

"You want?" Agnes said, handing me a coffee.

"Yeah, thanks." I was still staring at the barrette. "I need fuel for our fight."

"Will there be fighting?" She looked calm, even pleasant, turning to face me. She smelled faintly of Castile soap. There was something unusually still about her: no phone. She took her phone everywhere, set it next to her plate at the dinner table, propped it against the mirror when she flossed her teeth. She fell asleep with it in her hand and unlocked it with her thumbs as soon as she opened her eyes.

"Are you going to fight with me?" I said.

She put her fists up and jabbed lightly in my direction. There was a playfulness to her that I felt could only be attributed to having spent the weekend having sex.

"You tell me."

"Well. You did call my mother and sister and tell them you didn't know where I was."

"I was getting worried." She lowered her voice. "I also called Cash."

"And?"

"And he said you'd stopped by to see him."

I began to drive, taking a shortcut to the Mass Pike along back roads. It took only a few minutes to feel that we were out in the country: gray slush and dripping trees. Even the cleanest houses looked dirty outside in February in New England. In her lap, Agnes's hands began to twitch. Missing her phone, I thought.

"What else did Cash say?"

"Nothing. I don't know if you've ever noticed, but he's kind of boring, that Cash."

"Yeah."

Agnes sighed and slipped her arms out of the coat, drawing it around her as if it were a cloak.

"Thank you for picking me up," she said.

"Common courtesy."

We were approaching the lookout where I used to go with my father, where I had once run into Noel. I turned off the main road and onto the rocky, single-car lane.

"Where are we going?" she said.

"I want some fresh air."

"So open a window."

I parked by the tower. It was covered in graffiti, with torn paper and plastic bags scattered around its base.

"This looks a little grim," Agnes said.

"Just for a minute."

"I'll follow you anywhere, Zuzu."

"Except for the times you mysteriously disappear." I unbuckled my seat belt and got out of the car.

"I didn't 'mysteriously disappear,'" she said, getting out after me. She shut the door on her seat belt, and she had to open it and fix the belt and shut it again. "*You* did."

The stairs were smaller than I recalled, the space between the railings narrower than in my memory. We went single file. I was sweaty by the time we reached the top.

"This must be gorgeous in October," Agnes said, wrapping her hands around the railing. "I thought there might be one of those coin-operated binocular things up here."

"Nope."

"Okay." She beat lightly on the railing with her palms. "So what are we doing here?"

"Thinking."

"About?"

"I don't know. Everything."

"Sounds dramatic." She made a clicking sound with her tongue against her teeth. "Here's a question. Why'd you leave me at Heidi's?"

"I didn't leave."

"Oh, yes, you left me at Heidi's."

"I couldn't find you anywhere," I said.

"I was there."

"But you weren't."

"You couldn't find me. Doesn't mean I wasn't there."

I stared at her.

"Is this like one of your logic games or whatever?"

She tucked her hair behind her ears. Her nose was starting to run in the cold. I thought of how often I had told her, early on, that she looked like a doll: There was no discord, no meaningful flaw, among her features. I had meant it as a rather astonished compliment, but she didn't like to hear it. *It sounds like you're saying I look mass-produced.*

"Do you know how it *felt* to call Cash?" Agnes looked up at the sky, hands clasped at her heart. She used the same squeaky, high-pitched voice she used to imitate the nervous summer associates who flooded her office each June. "Sir? Do you know where my wife is?"

I shoved my hands into my pockets.

"Okay, stop," I said.

"Did you even *try*, sir?"

"Oh, my God. *Stop.*"

"He didn't try?"

"Agnes."

"That's a no." She turned and leaned over the railing, leaning far enough for her boots to lift off the metal platform. I recalled lying next to her years ago, both of us feeling confessional, trying to find ways to bare more, to offer more. We traded fears: She claimed that one of hers was falling from a great height. I told her the truth: My fear was to be found undesirable.

"It wasn't like that," I said. She was still leaning over the bar.

"He said you had a drink at a hotel and then you left."

"That is accurate."

She shook her head.

"What?" I said. "I'm not allowed to have a drink?"

"My God. Have a dozen. Go for it."

"Then what were you hoping to hear?"

Her boots came back down, hard, and made a ringing sound.

"Let's go," she said. "Theresa's already on the way back from the Adirondacks. I don't want to be late for Gideon."

She led the way to the car, stopping at the trunk to pull her phone out of a zippered pocket in her bag. In the passenger seat, she seemed not to notice the cold as she typed. I felt that I recognized her more easily with her head tilted phoneward. I waited a full three minutes before starting the car.

"Nice to see you reunited with your lover," I said.

"What?" She looked up. "Are you kidding?"

"Not really."

"I have to answer emails. Every day. Without exception. Sorry."

"Doesn't bother me," I said, shifting into reverse. "The social media addiction, all your stupid newsletters? Those bother me."

"Stupid newsletters. Okay. So the one about local events that our son might like? Is that one stupid? Or vegetarian recipes, since you don't really eat meat—is that one stupid?"

"It's stupid that you'd rather look at those than talk to me. Ever."

"Yeah, okay. I never talk to you."

The tires spun, both in drive and in reverse. Agnes stared at her phone. I shifted into park and got out, circling the car, noting nothing unusual, just mud and chunks of ice. I knocked on her window.

"What," she said.

"I need help."

She climbed over the console and into the driver's seat and tried backing out of the spot. The tires spun, kicking up a spray of mud.

"What did you do, Zuzu," she said.

"Nothing. It's just stuck."

She got out, left the motor running, opened the trunk.

"I really don't have time for this," she said. There was a shoebox in the corner of the trunk: sneakers Agnes had bought herself, then deemed too ugly. She had said she'd return them several weeks earlier.

"Guess we're stuck with those now," I said.

"Whatever." She took off the lid, tore it in half, and wedged a half behind two of the tires.

"What exactly is the plan here?"

"Try now." She stepped back, her hands on her hips.

"But what does that even do?"

"I don't know. It's something other than mud." She nudged the driver's door with her foot. "Try it."

I got back in, shifted into reverse, and glided over the cardboard. The car spun a half circle and stopped, facing the rocky lane back to the main road. In the rearview mirror, I saw Agnes lean back and howl in triumph. She kicked her legs up in the air, collected the wet cardboard, then chased after me and let herself back into the car.

"Your cheeks are so red," I said.

"With glory, yeah." She pulled strands of hair from under the collar of her coat. "I can't believe it *worked*."

"You did it."

"It feels so good when something actually works." She laughed and sank lower into the seat. She closed her eyes. We drove in silence for roughly two minutes. When I took her hand, she pulled it away. "But seriously," she said, eyes still closed. "I think you need to maybe get over it with him already."

"There's nothing to get over. He's my friend."

"This whole denial bit is actually more insulting."

"It's not a bit."

She flicked a leaf from the laces of her left boot.

"Fine," I said. "I showed up at his door and threw myself at him."

"Even when you joke like that, you sound wistful," Agnes said.

I TRIED TO imagine a peaceful place for us. I conjured a table: glass-topped white iron, rocky outcropping, Atlantic casting up spray at our ankles, our son well-fed and happy in someone else's care. Just Agnes and Zuzu at an imaginary table. I could feel my elbows on the cold glass. We played a game, setting confessions down like so many interlocking pieces. One from me: I'm worried you don't want me anymore.

One from Agnes: Same.

I thought of how, during our first years in New York, I woke up to the self-important sound of her heels when she left for work. I tended to her blooming collection of expensive handbags; without them, she feared that she wouldn't be taken seriously at the office. She saved three hours on Sundays for herself—hot yoga, then a kombucha, then a long phone call to her parents in Marin. From what I could hear through the closed door, she impressed upon them that she was working hard. I knew them well enough to know that, in their way, they were suggesting she could work even harder.

In our first year together, in the apartment on Fourteenth Street, we turned her bedroom into an office, and she moved into my room. Her nightstand grew piles of magazines, days-old water glasses, butterfly clips and hand cream and candy bar wrappers, rubber bands everywhere. I loved her clutter. I didn't know how to love her without extending it to the strands of hair she left in her brush with the purple-tipped bristles. If she had done it, I loved it. If she said it, it seemed to me that it was right.

I didn't know this was unfair to both of us.

"I'm picturing us at a table," I told her. "Like right on the ocean."

"Sounds nice," she said. "You never want to go away with me though."

"I said I didn't want to go on *safari*. I'm sorry. I'm literally afraid of most animals."

"Zuzu," Agnes said, rolling her eyes.

"I *am*, though."

"Tell me what happens at the table on the ocean."

"Nothing good."

"Ha."

"Okay," I said. "At the table on the ocean, we are honest with each other."

"Hmm. I feel like we should try it out in a car, see how we do."

"All right."

"So tell me what you wish I'd say right now."

"I wish you would say, let's go clean out that storage unit and get home in time for Gideon."

"I'm feeling a little sad that this is your fantasy," she said, "but if it's really what you want, let's go."

The Project

I couldn't manage the padlock, and I had to hand the small key to Agnes.

"All yours," she said, pulling the metal door up by its handle.

"If it's all mine, I get to burn it."

"Yes, we know you hate possessions."

"Only most of them," I said.

I pressed the flashlight on my phone and swung the beam around. Boxes, neatly stacked. A cherry grandfather clock that Agnes's parents had given us when we were in law school. Its base was so broad that to accommodate it we'd had to push our love seat out at an angle.

"What is this? Paint?" Agnes lifted a can by the handle. "What were we going to paint?"

"I have no idea." I poked at an empty fishbowl with my toe. "We never had a fish, so I don't know what this is about, either."

She stopped to run her hand along the grain of the grandfather clock. "Shouldn't this have been wrapped in something?"

"Probably. We didn't know what we were doing back then."

"Do we know now?" She shivered and stamped her feet. We could see our breath. Across the way, someone else unlocked their unit and began loading boxes onto a dolly. They turned on music, setting it to an unapologetic volume before wheeling the dolly away. I'd paid for unlimited access to a communal garbage container when we arrived, and I figured that most of our items would end up in there.

"We need to move faster," I said. "I'm really cold."

She dropped a small broom-and-dustpan set onto the floor and frowned at me.

"Are you going to complain the whole time?"

"Maybe," I said.

"You're the one who desperately wanted to come here. So you have to be happy."

"I'm happy, I'm happy," I said.

A 2011 CALENDAR from a botanical garden (gift from Heidi?). A faux-Wedgwood tea service we'd found at a yard sale. The calligraphy set Agnes bought for fun and never even opened. We'd stood in Pearl Paint for fifteen minutes, comparing two similar sets while I teased her for taking so long. I was six months pregnant with Gideon, and all I cared about was the ramen we were planning to have after we finished our errands. I recall blowing on a spoonful of broth when she told me she was planning to make our baby's birth announcements by hand, instead of getting them printed. I told her I didn't think she would really have time for that, which turned out to be true, but she said, "I want to try," and I remember hearing the sweetness and aspiration in it.

"What about this?" I said, holding up the box. I saw her throat tightening with the instinct to keep it, just because it was there, and because it still functioned.

"Toss it," she said.

A gift to me.

"You're not going to want these," she said, holding up a box. "It's just CDs."

"Let me see."

Every single one of them was from Cash, who had dated the discs in his wobbly handwriting. He'd made me a birthday mix for nine years in a row, right up until the year I got married.

"I'll toss them," I said. I surprised myself by actually tossing them.

We weren't talking much as we worked. We were both aware of the limited possibilities. Sometimes, watching Agnes shake a box before she opened it, I was certain that she had slept with Heidi. A minute later, watching her retie her shoe, I thought, *She would never.*

I WAS TIRING of our project and its hairpin turns: sadness when I found a rose-shaped enamel trivet that Agnes had given me, afraid that I would mock it (I didn't), for Valentine's Day; irritation at the sight of tennis rackets we'd never used. I took an abandoned dolly, loaded it with stuff, and brought it to the trash. I made four trips, feeling industrious and bold. We sold the clock for a tenth of what it was probably worth, cash, to the guy with the unit across from ours.

I remembered that we did, in fact, have a fish, during the months I studied for my second try at the bar exam. I had complained, to Agnes, that I couldn't think about anything else; that I was consumed, not so much by the exam questions themselves, but by what it would mean about me if I still didn't pass.

"It would mean you try again," she'd said.

She brought home a purple betta fish and set it on the table next to a stack of study guides. We named it Tab, short for Take-a-Break. I cannot remember, now, how long the fish was with us. I do remember feeding it, and sometimes cleaning the neon blue gravel we'd scattered at the bottom of the bowl. For a brief time we had a small mirror we could attach to the bowl to watch Tab react, gearing itself up for a fight with its own reflection, but Agnes found out that these were considered cruel—we'd had no idea—and she threw the mirror out.

"I HATE TO open this," she said, hoisting up a vacuum-sealed bag of clothing, "but I want to see if your dad's old sweatshirt is in here."

I touched my throat, knowing my nervousness could be mistaken for grief.

"No idea," I said.

She pulled out a lime-green miniskirt and frowned at it.

"I feel like a stranger's stuff got mixed up with ours."

"Maybe," I said.

"I'm kidding. I just can't believe how much we managed to accumulate when we were so young. It's kind of gross."

I nodded. She dropped the heavy bag of clothes, and came over to stand next to me.

"You look like you're going to throw up," she said. "You okay?"

I nodded again, but when she suggested I sit, I sat on the filthy concrete floor and leaned against her.

"You used to talk about that sweatshirt a lot," she said.

"Well, I don't think it's here."

"You think it's at home?"

I thought it was on a bench at a hotel she'd never stood inside. I thought it would make its way to a lost-and-found box, and that after going unclaimed for weeks, it would wind up in a trash bin. Cash, who had intermittently forgotten about my sweatshirt for years, would never think of it again. My wife, searching for it in the dim light of the storage unit, would forget about it too.

I regretted the physical loss of it. I liked its softness and its shape, its familiar holes and tears, the way I pinched the cuffs under my fingers, the way I shuffled when I wore it, sinking into its warmth, into a youthful posture that was otherwise inaccessible to me. A daydreamy slouch with a drink and a mixtape, no worries of any real substance, the sleeves trailing loose threads when I gestured—I'd left it, it was gone.

"Who knows where it is," I said. Agnes was already standing up, moving on. The dolly was loaded with things to get rid of, and she hauled it away.

How Time Works

September 5, 2000

When he tilts his head to let the orange roll into the space you make with your body, let it fall. You don't care about the orange and neither does he. You care that the veins in his arms stand out, you care that your impulse to touch them is so strong you have to tell yourself *no*. Already, you want to keep him for yourself. If you could get him to walk through the gates with you, you could leave this school together. You could board a train and find out where it was going once it arrived.

Decide you will not pretend about anything. Do not try to imitate girls who walk the earth with casual disinterest; you have no such thing. You are all interest, you are made of it. Five months from now, at a concert in the chapel to your left, he will place his hand on the back of your neck, and you will not know if it is a casual gesture of affection. Here is the thing to understand about you and your friend Cash: This will never be casual for you.

It won't be casual, but you won't board a train today. You are responsible, both of you. You packed vitamins and floss. You both have new checkbooks, which you balance by hand with a pen. You will stand there, and the orange will move from him to you to him. You will want to stand there with him long after it is time to go.

Acknowledgments

Enormous gratitude to Claudia Ballard, a dream agent: insightful, diligent, encouraging, brilliant. Thank you to Alison Fairbrother for wise and perceptive editing, and to everyone at Riverhead. Thank you to Fiona Baird. Thank you to Isabel Wall and Poppy Hampson for such enthusiasm for this book, and to the entire Viking team. Thank you to MacDowell, the Fine Arts Work Center, Ucross, Yaddo, the Constance Saltonstall Foundation for the Arts, and the Wallace Stegner Fellowship at Stanford University.

Thank you to Andrew Meredith and Jessica Grose, superb writers and advice givers, and dear lifelong friends.

Thank you to Wesley Gibson, Roger Skillings, and Paul La Farge, beloved late writing teachers, joyfully remembered.

Thank you to Emily Weinstein for sharing in the exhilaration of our Thursday Gibson class.

Thank you to Paul Kane for years of unwavering encouragement.

Thank you to Tom Jenks and Carol Edgarian at *Narrative*, and to Patrick Ryan at *One Story*.

ACKNOWLEDGMENTS

Thank you, M, for more than can possibly fit on these pages, and for believing since Helen.

Thank you to L and A, inspiring artists and writers, paragons of kindness.

M, L, and A: I love you infinitely.